The Brainless Beauty

EMMANUEL KELECHI EGBUGARA

ISBN
978-1-958122-14-3 (Paperback)
978-1-958122-13-6 (eBook)
978-1-958122-15-0 (Hardcover)

Dedication

To Alexander O. Egbugara

Whose Inspiring Life Serves
Notice to the World
That God Is Faithful and True

Table of Contents

Chapter One...1

Chapter Two 21

Chapter Three 33

Chapter Four..53

Chapter Five 71

Chapter Six...87

Chapter Seven 97

Chapter Eight 119

Chapter Nine 127

Chapter Ten 141

Acknowledgements

It's good nurture to be grateful no matter how great or small a kindness. Therefore, to all those who in one way or the other have made positive contributions to my life, I say thank you *and God bless.*

To my mother, Madam Charity E. Egbugara, and my siblings, Deaconess Christabel Ebelebe, Brothers Victor, Emeka, Godsmind, let the love of Christ Jesus prosper us unto eternity.

Special thanks and love to my beloved wife, Ifeoma, for reviewing patiently and dedicatedly and typesetting this work with me. God bless you, Enyi.

Chapter One

To the star fields and the sea of diamonds, to the gold fields of sky horizons, and the beautiful setting sun, even the rumbling nimbus of the blue sky, the reapers are imaginations.

As the stretched hand of the breeze caresses and the whirlwind blows her whistles, these we appreciate by feelings but better enhanced by imagination, only when we stand with nature, *belonged.*

The afternoon was very hot as expected at this time of the year in the tropical region of Africa. The rainy season was gradually eroding away the dry season at this time of October, in particular in Lagos, where the weather condition was different from other parts of Nigeria, may be because of its geographical location of being close to the Atlantic Ocean. Hence, even if the sun was right up there at the equator, the breeze from the sea intermittently cruised in the atmosphere, soothing the inhabitants. And Victoria Island was the right place to be at this particular moment. Ugomma's parents lived in this locality.

'Ugomma, what time is your flight? I suppose it's by 2 p.m.'

'No, Mum, it's at exactly 3.30 p.m. The ADC (Aviation Development Company) airline will be departing Ikeja local airport for Calabar, the capital city of Cross River State.'

Ah, your father phoned from his office about twenty minutes ago that he has fixed other necessary documents for the journey. However, he will be home soon for the family's get-together before seeing you off to the airport. I hope you have readily packed your luggage, and ensure not to forget any important thing behind, especially, your personal effects, okay?'

'Yes, Mum! You know, I started arranging and packing my belongings these past two days, invariably. There is no reason why I should forget anything behind.'

'Who is there?' Mrs Uboma asked. 'Maarako, can't you hear the horn of your father's car? Go quickly and open the gate for him. Yeah, that reminds me, where has the security man gone to?'

Ugomma answered, 'Mum, Sule took his child who suddenly took ill to the hospital.'

'That is all right,' she responded to her daughter.

A few minutes later, Mr Fredrick entered the house. 'Welcome, darling, how was your day at work?' Mrs Uboma enquired.

'Oh fine, Lolo. You smell nice. I like the fragrance of your perfume he complimented her. 'You know, because of Ugomma's journey to Calabar this afternoon, I had to conclude every other engagement that demanded my urgent attention because I have decided taking our daughter there, personally? As he told his wife the latest plan, he called their youngest son, 'Uchendu!'

'Yes, Daddy?' he answered.

'Go to the driver and inform him to drive out the Toyota land cruiser jeep from the garage, which is the car we will use to go to the airport in the next hour, okay?'

'Yes, Daddy,' he responded and hastened to the driver's quarter.

'Ugomma!'

'Yes, Daddy,' she responded.

'I hope everything is actually in order?' he enquired. And she answered in the affirmative while welcoming her father. 'I contacted my friend, Mr Benjamin Ekong, that we are arriving in Uyo this evening, about 5.30 p.m., since the ADC Airline has got provision for an air-conditioned bus that conveys passengers straight to Uyo from Calabar airport. Even then, the distance from Calabar to Uyo could be covered within one hour, forty-five minutes. Mr Ekong will be waiting there to drive us to his home at Ewet Housing Estate. And of course, his family will be waiting to receive us too.'

'O, darling, that's a good arrangement. I do remember Benjamin, your friend and fellow alumni at the University of Lagos, in those good old days,' his wife interjected.

'Yea, you know, after returning from Germany, Benjamin established an engineering firm down home which handles lots of contracting jobs for Mobil Producing Unlimited at Eket and ASCON (Aluminium Smelting Company of Nigeria) at Ikot Abasi, all in Akwa Ibom, his home state. In fact the old boy is doing marvellously well now.'

Then entered Uchendu, and his father enquired whether he had informed the driver. 'Yes, Daddy, Uncle Ephraim is taking his bath and will get the car ready at the soonest.'

'That's all right,' responded Igwe Uboma.

'Lunch is ready,' announced Mrs Uboma. 'Felicia, take some food to Ephraim, the driver, and join us at the table.'

'Yes, ma,' responded the house girl.

'Em! Beloved, the aroma of this egusi soup and pounded yam has aroused my appetite. This delicacy must have been prepared especially to celebrate your daughter becoming a university undergraduate?

'Yes, O Igwe, my only daughter is going away, so I have to give her a "treat", jare.'

'Thanks, Mum, for caring Ugomma said.

'You are welcome, darling replied her mother. Igwe opened a bottle of wine, and they all toasted to the good health and God's guidance for Ugomma; clinking their glasses while saying 'cheers, cheers', they all celebrated.

After the meal, when it was time to go, Ugomma called together her younger brothers—Maraako and Uchendu. 'You guys should not fight O. Study hard and don't stress Mum. Be good boys, okay?'

'Okay, Sister they chorused.

Maraako reminded her, 'Ugo, what about that thing you promised me?'

'Yes, Maraako, I kept them on my dressing table. Give the other package to Uchendu, okay?'

'Thank you, Sister Ugo said the duo joyfully.

'You are both welcome she responded.

'Felicia, who is at the gate?' Igwe enquired.

'It's Sule, sir. He's just returned from the hospital she responded.

'Hospital? Why?'

Lolo answered, 'Darling, his child took ill around noon and was rushed to the hospital. Meanwhile, I phoned Dr Michael to take good care of the child.'

'Oh sure, Mike knows his way with children, no problem,' Igwe added.

Instantaneously, Sule entered the house and greeted his employer. 'Good afternoon, sir.'

'Yes, Sule, I learnt you took your child to the hospital. How is he?'

'He is well now. Thank you, sir and ma.'

Sule went to Ugomma. 'I hope you are ready. Honestly, we will miss you O!'

'*Haba,* Mr Sule, that will not be for too long. I will be around for the Christmas holidays. Take good care of your family. Please give this toy to Ibrahim, my little friend.'

'Ah! Thank you and goodbye.'

'Darling, it's about time you people should get going in order to meet the flight schedule suggested Mrs Uboma.

'That's right, Mum responded Ugomma as she called her younger brother to help carry her luggage into the car.

After stacking the luggage into the car, Igwe informed his wife that he would be back in Lagos on Monday. 'Goodbye, darling, and take care of the family.'

Ugomma popping her face out from the car cheered her brothers and said, 'Mummy, I will phone you after registering my courses, though I heard it is a tedious exercise.'

'Don't worry, you will accomplish that as well, but be very prayerful.'

Hajiya, Sule's wife, waved to Ugomma and said, 'I wish you safe journey O!'

'Thank you, Hajiya. Take care of your children.'

Ephraim informed Sule as the latter opened the gate. 'I will be back soon depending on the traffic.'

'Okay, Ephraim, no problem, bye-bye.'

On their way to the airport, Igwe and his daughter engaged into a discussion. 'Daddy, how developed is Calabar?'

'The town was the first capital city of Nigeria during the colonial era before the capital was relocated to Lagos and now Abuja. In fact, the metamorphosis of Nigeria's capital city is just like the United States of America, from Philadelphia to New York and now Washington DC. The contemporary Calabar town is developing fast because of the Export Processing Zone project which the Federal Government of Nigeria sited there. The project will primarily handle the processing and export activities of raw materials abroad and also help decongest the ports in Lagos Apapa and Tin-Can seaports as well as Port Harcourt port. So there are a lot of business activities going on at Calabar right now.'

Looking at the clock, Igwe said to his driver, 'Ephraim, you should accelerate the car if we must catch that flight?

'Okay, sir,' he replied and sped off.

'Ugomma!'

'Yes, Daddy.'

Igwe advised his daughter, 'You know, from now you have become an independent adult. That means you will be deciding on vital issues of your life, whether to achieve academic excellence and propagate the good name of the family or join the bad and unserious friends and jeopardise your future career and destiny. I remember in those years in University of Lagos, as an undergraduate, some girls from rich homes were carried away by the euphoria of being in the university. Before you knew it, they were embarrassed with failures and "carry over"?

'Daddy, what is carry over?' Ugomma asked.

'This is failed course(s) that a student must repeat and pass before he is allowed to register and study subsequent course(s). This is because the school curriculum is planned sequentially from the known to the unknown. The number of courses and credit units of study increases every semester. So long as the student cannot pass those courses, it poses academic danger or threat for the student. Where adequate care is not taken through hard work, the studentship of the person will be withdrawn by the university authority and he will be advised to withdraw in his own interest. This is referred to as *rustication!*

'Eh-eh? Ugomma exclaimed.

'You see, my daughter, your primary objective of going to the University of Uyo is to achieve academic prowess, qualify as a graduate, and proceed further to the Nigeria Law School, after which you will be called to bar. Then as a qualified legal practitioner, you can effectively take care of my business empire.'

'Ah, Daddy, that will be very great,' Ugomma added.

'Yes, my dear, that's why you must not lose focus, okay?'

'Yes, Daddy,' she responded.

Reaching the airport, Igwe spoke further; Ephraim had parked the car somewhere out there. 'Thank God there was no traffic jam this afternoon. My fear was that Maryland and Onigbogbo junction.'

'Oga, at this time of the day, traffic is usually light, especially coming through the third mainland bridge via Oworonshoki and Oshodi-oke axis, straight to the airport,' his driver added.

'That is true, Ephraim, but one cannot predict the traffic in Lagos, considering the bad roads full of potholes and gullies and the menace of tankers trailers.

'One wonders if the officials of FERMA, Ministry of Works, and other related authorities are lying in oblivious doldrums or they do not use these roads. Well, that is Nigeria for you,' concluded Igwe.

As they were taking out their luggage from the car, an old friend of Igwe accosted them. 'Ah, Igwe! What brought you to the airport? Are you travelling home again so soon?'

'O mine, Nze Duru, good seeing you again. I and my daughter are travelling to Uyo through Calabar airport. She has been offered a provisional admission at the University of Uyo to study law.'

'That is beautiful,' commended Nze Duru, stretching out his hands to congratulate Ugomma. 'She has also blossomed into a more beautiful young woman than her mother reiterated Nze. Ugomma greeted him, blushing and thanking him for the remarks.

'Well, Igwe, when are you expected back at Lagos? There were salient issues raised at the last meeting that I would want to discuss about.'

'Em! Hopefully by Monday evening I should be back at Lagos responded Igwe.

'Then I will see you in the office on Tuesday afternoon. Do have a safe journey Nze wished them, stepping aside.

'Okay, see you then, thanks.'

As they entered the departure hall, an announcement came through the speaker: 'All passengers travelling to Calabar with the ADC Airline are requested to check in and board the aircraft which will be taking off for destination in the next five minutes, thank you.'

Igwe and Ugomma joined the other boarding passengers who climbed on to the plane. They sat in a twin seater. Ugomma sat next to the window from where she could have a clear view of the landscape. Then the speaker buzzed. 'Ladies and gentlemen, you are all welcome on board. This is ADC, your friendly and reliable airline. Please put on your safety belt and study the safety guidelines in front of you, in case of an emergency. However, we expect to have a smooth flight to Calabar in the next couple of hours. Relax and enjoy the flight, thank you.' The plane's engine then roared, taxied along the tarmac, and gathered momentum before heaving up into the clouds.

Once airborne, Ugomma, who was travelling by air for the first time, was captivated by the sight of the beautiful horizons and layers of purified nimbus of the clouds. She commented the same to her father, 'Daddy, the horizon looks white and pure, so beautiful, it captivates my soul.'

'Yes, my daughter, nature is so gorgeously beautiful. On one of my various trips to Port Harcourt, I saw a similar sight which kept me wondering. I marvelled at Providence. The wonderful handiwork of God cannot be comprehended by any mortal soul. Nobody can fathom the in-depth beauty that nature has bestowed on human environment. The problem with man is that we are so mundane, entrenched in pursuit of earthly vain glories, forgetting the *very essence of our beings* and purpose of living. That's why most people cannot achieve and maintain peace within and without no matter the situation they may find themselves because they have refused to learn, practice, and use the efficient control of the mind.

'We as human beings created in the image and likeness of God have spiritual capacity to know and understand God's voice, movement, and his presence in our lives. We also have the ability to renew our souls with the Word of God so as to be intuitive, imagine, reason, to remember and assert *our individuality which is the richest natural gift of Providence to man.* This transcends the frontiers of spiritual and physical dimension which grow in various proportions to the individual's level of awareness, aspirations, visions, and conformity to the natural laws and norms. The more attention we tenaciously give to the natural dimension, pursuing mundane things and vain glories, we really dwarf and becloud the spiritual man, our real selves. Relationship with God and man leads to the actualisation of man's very essence of existence and, hereafter, the *ultimate* goal.'

'Dad, you sound so philosophical and distinctively poetic,' observed Ugomma.

'Yes, my beloved daughter, over time, I have tried to discover myself so that I may know my ways, for this is important for any earth-ferrying man. In my solitude which I love dearly, I meditate on the working of nature so as to appreciate my environment the more, both spiritually and otherwise. There is a great challenge that puzzles my mind.'

'Yes, Dad, what is it?'

'It is the unpredictable disposition of man's characteristics behaviour. No wonder psychologists and social scientists affirm that you cannot claim to know any man so well. Because he is susceptible to change, man influences his environment and vice versa. Human beings are easily influenced by external factors because of lack of internal stability which only the Holy Spirit of God can activate. You see, the power of creation is nestled in man by God. Right from creation when God created man in the spiritual realm, he gave man an earthly form to live here on earth and God blessed man and said, "Go into the world and multiply, have dominion over all things, subdue and replenish the earth." But due to lack of God's knowledge, greed, and selfishness, man today are subduing by plundering and squandering our national wealth without replenishing and investing in the system. Rather, they cart away our God-given resources in Nigeria and stack them away in foreign lands and banks. Thereby, they are fugitives and vagabonds. Well, the judge will judge us some day.'

'Dad, 1 love the way you sing. The other night I heard you sing melodiously to Mum. That sounded purely from a beloved soul. Can I ever sing like you?'

'You can, Ugo, only if you can search deep into your soul. This talent runs in the family. The gene is nestled in you. You cannot discover it on the surface. Ask God to help you discover yourself through constant meditation on the Word, fasting, and fervent prayers. The source is the supreme God, the giver of every good thing. Always remember the golden motivator and facilitator of all times. Ask and you shall receive, seek and you shall find, knock and the door shall be opened unto you?

'Ladies and gentlemen, we have safely got to the Calabar airport. Welcome to Canaan city. Please fasten your seat belts as the plane will be landing in two minutes' time,' announced the pilot. Eventually the plane landed safely, and the passengers disembarked into the arrival hall.

Ugomma asked her father as they were collecting their luggage, 'Daddy, did the airline make arrangement for bus service to Uyo?'

'Yes, my dear, we would not have any need to hire a taxi.'

'Attention please! Ladies and gentlemen, you are welcome to the Canaan city. Passengers going to Uyo, please proceed to the ADC airline bus parked beside the gate for the remaining part of your journey. Welcome and God bless?

All the Uyo bound passengers along with their luggage finally boarded the bus. The driver announced, 'Welcome, ladies and gentlemen, the journey to Uyo from here is about one and half hours. But considering the terrible condition of our federal roads, especially in this part of Nigeria, we will be arriving Uyo latest in two hours?

'Daddy, I observe a solemn serenity around here. Even the weather seems friendly unlike Lagos's weather. I also notice that the people are caring?

'You know, Ugo, the problem with cosmopolitan city dwellers like Lagos is that they fantasise a lot. It becomes frustrating when they are unable to actualise such dreams or meet up within the shortest time frame, unlike in the countryside where people are closer to nature, enjoy all there is, even deep undisturbed sleep. So they tend to be more reflective and respond the same to their environment?

'Look, Dad, the sign post reads "Itam junction. Welcome to Uyo, the Land of Promise". So we have arrived. Thank God for journey's mercy?

'Yes, my daughter?

'Ladies and gentlemen, here we are—Barracks Road, the terminal point of the journey,' the driver announced. He also asked the bus conductor to bring down the luggage of the passengers while the area manager stood watching.

'Ah! Mr Fred Uboma, it is so nice seeing you again. You are welcome to Akwa Ibom State?

'Thank you, Mr Benjamin Ekong. It is also nice seeing you again. How is your family?'

'They are all fine and expecting you. This must be your daughter. Such a fine young lady.'

'Yes, my friend. Ugomma, meet Mr Benjamin Eking.'

'Good evening, sir.'

'Good evening, my daughter. It is my pleasure meeting you. So how are you?'

'I am fine, thank you, sir.'

'Fred, let's get you home. You look fagged out.'

'Oh boy! Thank God for the safe journey.' They packed their luggage into his car boot; the two men sitting in front and Ugomma in the back, then Mr Benjamin drove off.

'Benjamin, this is a clean Benz you have got here,' complimented Mr Fred. 'You must be doing fine out here.'

'Thanks, man,' responded Benjamin. 'Well, as a matter of fact, I am not complaining but only grateful to God that I decided to come home from Germany when I did and better still settling down here in my home state. It avails me of the opportunity of taking care of my aged parents who are enjoying their grandchildren now?

'That is wonderful responded Fred. 'You are a great guy. I had no doubt about your potentials right then at Unilag (University of Lagos) The ride was smooth and short as they got to Ewet Housing Estate, where Mrs Ekong and her children were waiting for them.

Udoh, Mr Benjamin's son, opened the gate, and his daddy drove the car in with their visitors. 'Welcome, sirs greeted Udoh while closing the gate behind them.

'So, Fred, here we are His wife rushed to welcome them. 'Ufan, meet Mr Fred Uboma, my friend and fellow alumni, the Akokite, and his lovely daughter, Ugomma. Benjamin introduced the visitors to his wife, and they all exchanged greetings.

'Good evening, Ma Ugomma greeted her.

'Welcome, my daughter, to the land of promise. And welcome, sir she greeted Mr Uboma as they all walked into the sitting room, carrying the Ubomas' luggage.

'Oh boy! This is a beautiful home commented Fred.

'Thanks responded Benjamin. 'This place is called Ewet Housing Estate. That house over there belongs to the ousted chief of the Nigerian Air Force. In fact, the cream of Akwa Ibom society live here?

'That's great. You rightly belong here, my friend added Fred.

'Ufan he implored his wife, 'please show them to their rooms. They are going to spend the weekend with us. On Monday, Mr Uboma will take his daughter to the campus for the necessary documentations.' That done, and having had their baths and feeling refreshed, they all came down to the dining table for dinner. Mrs Ekong had prepared special Ibibio delicacies which attracted commendation from her husband in the presence of their guests, who were eating 'edikai-kong' soup with fufu for the first time. The visitors enjoyed the meal and thanked her.

Two days later, Fred commended Benjamin, 'This weekend has been a pleasant one. I hope to reciprocate by inviting you to Lagos for a holiday, and I hope you will oblige me.'

'That will be okay, Fred.'

'We have to leave for the campus this morning and see what I can achieve before returning back to Lagos with the afternoon flight. Please do me this favour, Ben. Be the guardian of Ugomma. Please monitor and admonish her periodically.'

'Of course, she will be visiting here at will. My daughter, Mfon, is her course mate, and they share the same opportunities,' concluded Ben.

'Madam, accept my profound gratitude. You have been a wonderful hostess. I have really enjoyed my stay and will comment that to my wife when I get back to Lagos this evening.'

'Sir, you are welcome,' responded Mrs Ekong.

'Please take care of Ugomma,' Fred further pleaded.

'There is no problem. Mfon, her friend and course mate, is always available to assist her, even in getting acquainted with the environment,' she assured Fred.

'I will surely keep in touch,' said Fred.

'Okay, sir, and goodbye.' He waved to them as Mr Ekong engaged the gear and drove towards the gate. And off they went.

While driving to the heart of the town, Fred said, 'Ben, I suppose you could drop us off first at the bank for me to open an account for Ugomma so that remitting money to her will be easy.'

'That is all right, Fred. I suggest you use Eureka International Bank, which would afford her the proximity and better service as it is located on Ikot-Ekpene Road.'

'Okay, Ben? He dropped them and drove off.

Alone at the entrance of the bank, Ugomma told her father, 'Daddy, 1 appreciate all your love and care. 1 wonder what I would have done without your coming along with me. I promise not to let you down?

'Well, my dear, that is why I am your father,' he replied.

The transaction in the bank took them about twenty minutes, and they quickly moved into the campus and accomplished all the registration processes. 'Now that we have done this much, Ugo, I would want you to settle down fast. When you have been allocated to a hostel, call us on phone. Ensure being prudent with your resources, okay?'

'Yes, Daddy,' she responded.

'Every other thing have been arranged to make your stay here really comfortable, but always pray to God for guidance, okay?'

'Yes, Daddy, I will keep in touch?

'Goodbye, Ugomma, be a nice girl?

'O! I will, Daddy, trust me. Do send my love to Mummy, Maraako, and Uche. Bye-bye? They thereafter parted, and Mr Fred Uboma returned to Lagos as scheduled.

In the course of time during the first month of her stay in the university, Ugomma got acquainted with the environment and other important parts of the town. She made a couple of friends who easily and readily flocked around her, especially her course mates and roommates at female hostel W1 Room 10. Her closest acquaintances were Nnedinma Adiaotu, Yetunde Giwa, Fatima Yusuf, Obiageri Abueke, and Mfon Ekong (her first and closest friend).

During their induction course as freshers (newly admitted students) in the university, they were conducted round the important infrastructural facilities on the twin campuses, such as Aso Rock office building for senior lecturers in the social science faculty, the academic and commonwealth buildings where lectures were held, the medical centre, the main library building, the remedial block where prelim and diploma students held their lecture; the VC, Prof. Fola Lasisi, referred to them as 'pretenders on campus'. The bulk of them constituted the happening babes on campus because of their attitude and mode of dressing. There was also the Nigerian Postal Services Office on the main campus and the multi-purpose and banquet halls. There were hostels in both the main campus and the annex. The faculties of law, engineering, business administration, and agriculture were located on the annex campus while the faculties of natural and applied sciences, education, arts, pharmacy, etc were located on the main campus. The offices of the senate, vice chancellor, and other principal officers were on the main campus. Invariably, the seat of power was on the main campus of the University of Uyo. Habib Bank PLC was the official bank of the university and had its branch in the main campus, through which students paid their fees; salaries of academic and nonacademic staffers of the university were also paid through it.

Flowers like bride of Barbados, hibiscus, sun flower abounded on the main campus, whereas the whispering trees, queen of the night, the Canailles family, orange trees, etc were housed on the annex campus. The gate linking the twin campuses opened on to Ikpa Road, which was the university road joining Ikpa-Itu Road junction where retail market operated daily. At the end of this road was a diploma school of accountancy, its students imposing themselves as undergraduate students of UniUyo. There were also many supermarkets scattered all over the university environ owned by Igbo merchants, mainly patronised by the female students.

Lectures commenced in earnest with course assignments being given by lecturers who used it to sensitise the students on their primary objective of being in the university and not meshing in the euphoria of 'jambit-ship'. The male students, old in the system with all intrigues, started the 'October rush' of toasting and chasing the new female students, mesmerising the babes with words of 'sweet nonsense'. Consequently, upon returning after a long vacation fully loaded with resources, those male students could afford to flamboyantly show off and run after the babes. The old female students also showed off by dressing to kill, the 'notice me' fashion parade acquired during the holiday. This was actually the most vibrant period in the school system because the socio-economic status of the students activated ripple effects on the general economic activity of the university and the environs. Students were relaxed, radiating in good health, pomp and pageantry, happy reunion with fellas. There was resilience on the twin campuses. The hostels and classrooms were renovated during the vacation. Some students extended gifts to some of their lecturers both in kind and cash with the view of watering the ground so as to pass their course works.

The academic and non-academic staff busied themselves with their schedules and meetings, ready for full-blown academic activities. The older students with ease completed new semester course registrations; those having carried over juggled and jostled their new and old courses to accommodate the maximum allowed twenty-four credits units by the Nigerian University Commission, which posed a sense of reality on them as per the very need to work hard. The setting or scenario at this time in the campus was a rejuvenated youthful exuberance cutting across the strata of humanity within the whole environment.

The university authorities were doing their usual thing of induction and enculturation of the freshers into the system proper before their matriculation slotted for the second day of December. Letters of invitation were sent out to parents and guardians, friends of the university, paramount rulers of the state, the pro-chancellor who was the Eleke of Egbaland, Government of Akwa Ibom State, and other distinguished personalities from far and near, not to forget the Federal Government that usually sent her delegates.

'Ugomma, what are your plans concerning the forthcoming matriculation?' Mfon asked.

'My dear, I posted the invitation letter to my parents just yesterday through the DHL courier services. After the induction programme this afternoon, I went to NITEL at Brooks Street to confirm with my mother at home if the mail did arrive on time and she confirmed that it did around 10 a.m. So my folks are surely going to be present. Well, time flies and we have just two days left. Mfon, why don't we go and rent the gowns?'

'Why not? A stitch in time saves nine responded Mfon. 'More so, I learnt the earlier callers do have the opportunity of picking up the most decent and best fitted ones before the rush.'

And while they were going for the gowns, a guy accosted them. 'Hi, Ugomma, how are you doing?'

'I am fine, Tony. Meet my friend, Mfon.'

'Good afternoon, Mfon. I am Tony of the Political Science Department. It is a pleasure meeting you,' she replied.

'Ugomma, where are you babes heading up to?' he asked.

'We are going to hire the matric gowns and probably get them ready, if they are not in good shape. You know the matriculation is two days away,' responded Ugomma.

'That is great, my dear. You are a fast babe,' said Tony as he departed from them. 'So catch you in the evening.'

'That's all right. Bye,' replied Ugomma and Mfon.

'Ugomma, who is that guy?' Mfon asked.

'I met him yesterday evening at the convocation park in the main campus,' Ugomma answered.

'He is good looking, no doubt, but be careful with him,' advised Mfon.

'No qualms, Mfon,' responded Ugomma.

'Now that we have gotten the gowns, let's get going for dinner,' said Mfon.

'Okay,' responded Ugomma.

But as they entered their room, one of her room-mates shouted, 'Guess what?! Georgina came looking for you, Ugomma, while you two were away. And I could not tell her precisely of your whereabouts.'

'Oh thanks, Fatima. We had just gone to get the matriculation gowns. I hope she is gonna come back later?' Ugomma asked.

'Yes, she promised to do so,' Fatima replied.

'Mfon, take a good look at me. How does this gown fit me?'

' *Wa* O! Nitty-gritty, you know, Ugomma, whatever clothes you put on fits you very well. The gown looks good on you, but we have to wash and iron them.'

'Yours look good also,' observed Ugomma. 'Meanwhile, can we have that orange juice please?' Ugomma asked Mfon. 'Fatima, come and share with us. Dora, you are also invited to share with us.'

'Sure, I don't mind, thank you,' responded the latter.

'There was a knock at the door,' said Mfon.

'Yes, come in if you are good looking,' responded Fatima jokingly.

'Hi, Ugomma,' Georgina greeted as she made her way into the room.

'Hi, Georgina, I learnt you had been here before. I and Mfon went to collect our matric gowns. Here they are.'

'That is fine,' responded Georgina.

'Please join us for a drink,' said Mfon while stretching out the bottle of juice to her.

'Thank you,' replied Georgina as she collected the bottle from Mfon.

Ugomma said, 'Mfon, let's go and shower while Georgina waits for us. Girls, stay cool and enjoy the music of Elton John—'Sacrifice'. In fact, I like listening to this track.'

'Same with me,' said Mfon. They left for the bathroom gisting.

'Mfon, do you know that I feel great about what is happening around me now? It is a dream come true. As an undergraduate, there is nothing I ask from my parents that will not be granted, more so, as their only daughter.'

'When are they arriving for the occasion?' Mfon asked.

'Tomorrow afternoon by four,' replied Ugomma. 'I think your daddy will wait for them at the ADC office at Barracks Road.'

'That is fine. I will then meet and know you mother. She must be a pretty woman,' said Mfon.

'Yes, she is. Let's get out of here. Georgina must be tired of waiting for us,' reasoned Ugomma.

'That is true agreed Mfon as they hurried out of the bathroom.

'Hi, Georgina, sorry that we kept you waiting. Kindly spare us a couple of minutes more and we shall go for dinner together.'

'Where are we having dinner?' Georgina asked.

'Udo-ette, of course,' replied Ugomma.

'Oh, that is all right by me,' said Georgina.

'Mfon, I am ready. Shall we go?'

'Yes, please, I am ready too,' responded Mfon.

Ugomma asked, 'Mfon, what is the time?'

'It's about 6.15 p.m.,' she responded.

'Look, ladies, this restaurant is crowded. Let us check out other "joints" further down.'

'Okay,' the duo responded as they moved towards Ekaette's cafe.

'You are welcome to Ekaette's cafe,' greeted the owner of the canteen.

'Good evening, madam,' they chorused.

'What can we offer you, my friends?'

'Please give me rice, fried plantain, and two pieces of meat,' Ugomma responded. 'Place your orders girls.' Mfon and Georgina asked the madam for the same order as Ugomma's.

As they were eating, Georgina asked, 'Girls, how has it been with your studies and other issues today?'

'Well, quite hectic but interesting. I see and regard each passing day on this campus as exciting and challenging, replied Ugomma as she turned to the food vendor. 'Please get us three bottles of coke drink, and let's have the bill for three of us.'

'Each plate of food is fifty naira plus sixty naira for the coke drink, totalling 210 naira only,' responded Madam Ekaette.

'Let us go, ladies,' urged Ugomma after settling the bill.

'Goodbye, my friends, and thanks for patronising us. See you tomorrow.'

'Good night, madam. We enjoyed your food.' They left and entered the campus through the gate of the annex campus.

As they approached Hostel W4, they ran into Tony and his friend Emeka, who had waited for Ugomma in her room for about fifteen minutes before they left. 'Hi, Tony, where are you going to?' Ugomma asked.

'I am going back to my hostel, of course,' responded Tony in an offhand tone indicating mixed annoyance and disappointment. 'However, meet Emeka. He is my course mate, room-mate, and my close friend.'

Ugomma shook hands with Emeka and said, 'It's my pleasure meeting you.'

'Mine also meeting you, Ugomma,' Emeka responded. After exchanging pleasantries and introducing both Georgina and Mfon, Tony and Emeka parted from the ladies but not before Tony and Ugomma had shared a brief personal discussion. Thereafter, Ugomma and Mfon accompanied Georgina to her residence in Hostel W4 Room 26.

'Tony! That is a great girl you have got there. How did you meet her?' Emeka asked as they entered their room.

'Boy! You know, experience, they say, is the best teacher,' replied Tony. 'I was standing in front of the department the other day under the "wisdom" tree when this elegant beauty was walking through the convocation park. I rightly assumed she is a "fresher". You know how they walk, as if they are afraid of the ground and their shadows, shy but apprehensive of the environment. That was the "go get her" signal. You know, I allowed her some distance, then followed up and walked beside her. I chat her up by adoring her beauty. You know women, and they like and flourish with flattery. Without much ado, she opened up, and we started discussing and strolling down to annex campus where she resides in Hostel W3 Room 10. She made me understand that she comes from a socio-economic well-to-do family.'

'That is great, boy,' shouted Emeka, who said that he had observed some other things about Ugomma. 'She seems to be arrogant and may lack the needed adoring composure that matters most, but gracefully carries herself. You know "beauty without brain is an illusion that leads to derision" and worst still in a society of make-believe, where people thrive in falsehood, affluence, lacklustre norms and values.'

'You see, Emeka, I love your sense of judgment and your analytical mind is sharp and starting without sentiment. I can always count on you as a good friend. Nevertheless, I am going to frazzle her before she knows it. Witty-natty putting my act together gets the job easily done.'

'Tony, did you observe her friend Mfon? She looks calm and intelligent, speaks coolly and calculative. That makes up for her beauty. In fact, she is my kind of girl—meek.'

'Why don't you go for her? I think both of you can flow together naturally.'

'I think you are right.'

'We shall join them at the matric party in their room on Friday evening,' said Tony.

'Okay,' responded Emeka.

'Well, girls, here we are declared Georgina as they entered her room. 'Ugomma, I presume Tony is your boyfriend. What is his department?'

'You are right, Georgina. He is in the Political Science Department—300 levels, the same as Emeka, his friend.'

'I like Emeka's sense of humour,' interjected Mfon. 'And he speaks fine, too.'

'Yes, I agree with you said Georgina.

'We should take our leave, Georgina. I am beginning to feel sleepy said Ugomma.

'I too chorused Mfon and Georgina. The duo were seen off till the hall's common room, and Mfon and Ugomma went back to their room and crashed on their beds, dozing off till the next morning.

Chapter Two

Ugomma, good morning! What time did you say your parents are arriving Uyo?'

'Fine morning to you, Mfon. I guess they should be here by 4 p.m. and your parents will be taking them to your house?

'I know. I asked for emphasis so that we hurry up with our engagements this morning, attend the only lecture for the day between 10 a.m. to 12 noon and go straight to Ewet so as to help in preparation for their reception?

'That is a great idea, Mfon. That's why I love you. You are so meticulous and deliberate in doing things. I wish I could share those qualities?

'Oh, well! Ugomma, thanks for flattering me?

'No,' protested Ugomma, 'you know that I am forthright?

'Yes, replied Mfon.Thanks all the same.

'That's better responded Ugomma. After the morning chores, they left for the lecture that got over by 12.30 p.m. and then went back to the hostel for the final preparation of the D-day the next day— the matriculation on 2 December. Meanwhile, all other freshers, on the two campuses and those living off campus, were caught up in the frenzy of preparing for the celebration slotted to kick off at 10 a.m. at the mini stadium of the university, where the parade proceedings and swearing in would take place. The non-academic staff on whose shoulders rested squarely the responsibility of organising the occasion were also busy, working tirelessly to ensure no hitches cropped up as directed by the vice-chancellor of the university, Prof. Foal Lassie.

At exactly 2.30 p.m., Mfon and Ugomma arrived at Mfon's home Ewet Housing Estate. 'Good afternoon, Mum chorused the duo.

'You are welcome, my daughters. I had expected both of you before now to help prepare for the arrival of Ugomma's parents, but not to worry. Everything has been taken care of.'

'Thanks, Mum chorused the duo.

'We were preoccupied with the activities in the campus, as everyone, especially the freshers, are busy putting the last touches for the occasion tomorrow explaining Mfon.

'That's all right responded her mother. 'In a little while now, your daddy will arrive from the office, and we will drive down to Barracks Road, ADC office, to bring home Ugomma's parents.'

'Okay, Mum chorused the girls.

'Put their room in order, Mfon, and Ugomma, clean up the kitchen she instructed as she climbed the stairs to her room to dress up before her husband came back.

'Welcome, Daddy greeted his son as he opened the gate for him to drive into the compound. On entering the sitting room, the girls welcomed him.

'Where is your mother, Mfon?'

'She is upstairs, Daddy she replied.

'Ah! Ugomma, how are you and how are you two getting on with your studies? And the preparation for tomorrow's occasion? I hope you are ready.'

'Fine, sir Ugomma responded.

'That's all right.'

The wife walked in. 'Eme-yong, how was your day in the office?'

'Okay, darling.' They hugged and kissed each other. 'My friend, Fred, and his wife will soon get to Uyo. He phoned me from the local airport, Calabar said her husband.

'Okay, dear, let's go for them.' Down they went in the car and drove off while the girls remained in the house.

Five minutes after they got to the ADC office at Barracks Road, the airline bus arrived from Calabar with Ugomma's parents and their last child, Uchendu. 'What a wonderful happy reunion!' exclaimed Fred Uboma as he embraced his friend Ben Ekong. They introduced their wives who were meeting for the first time beside seeing each other's picture previously. Mrs Ihuoma Uboma and Mrs Emem Ekong hugged each other and exchanged pleasantries. Without wasting much time, Uchendu, who was temporarily isolated, was also introduced to the Ekongs, who also accorded him recognition and hospitality. With their luggage docked in the boot of the Benz car, off they drove with Mr Ekong perfectly behind the wheels, manoeuvring the traffic which suddenly had become heavy because of the matriculation the next day, which had attracted lots of people from far and near. The whole town had become a beehive of activities. Trust the motorcyclists, locally called 'okada', for their daring runs. There was one common feature about these okada riders; they seemed possessed and controlled by the same mundane spirit of a frenzy quest for money, and they forgot the value of human life, observed Mrs Uboma. Her co-passengers in the car agreed with her. The situation had become the worst since the advent of retrenchment due to recession in the economy. Many people had lost their jobs and had to sustain their families through this option.

'Well, you can't blame them said Mrs Ekong.

'Even at that opined Mr Uboma, 'there is something wrong with the way they go about it. Greed is the name of the game.'

'I totally agree with you, my friend responded Mr Ekong.

'Eventually, ladies and gentleman, we are home. Welcome, Fred and family.' Ntekpere, Ben's elder son, came out at the blast of his father's car horn and threw open the gate wide and let them in; the two girls also rushed outside to welcome the August party. Pleasantries rent the atmosphere and environment. The household immediately was engulfed in a party mood. Notwithstanding, the obvious introductions were formerly done with pride and pageantry.

Supper was immediately served at the dining table. Mr Ekong, the jolly and jovial man he was, did not disappoint in taking control of conducting the August gathering. In fact, Fred, I was taken aback by the beauty of your lovely wife, Ihuoma. She appears more beautiful than what the picture depicted.' Ihuoma naturally blushed, as her husband Fred thanked Ben for the compliments.

Mrs Ekong interjected, 1 wondered at Ugomma's good looks, but that is a far cry from yours, madam.'

'Thank you, my dear,' responded Mrs Uboma happily. At one corner of the table, Uchendu, who was seated beside his sister, Ugomma, was babbling away about stories of Lagos. As they finished their meal and chatted over their drinks, Mfon, who naturally liked Uchendu, was also engrossed in the discussion between Ugomma and Uchendu, while the adults were in their own world.

Thereafter, the Ubomas were shown their lodgings by Mrs Ekong. Ugomma gisted with her parents when she received her gifts, including the ones from Ebuka, her elder brother at the University of Nigeria, Nsukka, studying electrical and electronics engineering. Also her immediate younger brother, Maraako, in Kings College, Lagos, had sent her something. After arrangements were made the occasion for the next day, both Mfon and Ugomma returned back to the campus at about 8 p.m. The girls reached their room to see it agog in party mood, as their room-mates were testing the best clothing for next day's occasion. The older students cheered the freshers nostalgically but pointed out to them that the fun fare was worth it while considering the hassles in passing the JAMB (Joint Admission and Matriculation Board) examination as thousands out there were not lucky enough to make it into the university. However, the ultimate was the final graduation at the end of it all.

'Fatima, have your parents arrived?' Ugomma asked from her corner.

'No,' she replied, 'they won't be coming in from Jos because of the distance. Rather, my uncle, who is a custom officer serving here in Uyo, will be coming with his wife.'

Yetunde interjected, 'Ugo, my parents arrived this evening from Lagos.'

'Ah! That's beautiful. My parents also came in from Lagos today,' responded Ugomma. That night, the girls hardly slept as they were caught up in excitement and greater expectations. But towards the wee hours of the dawning, they all lay down with the expectation of catching some sleep.

And so they woke up with a start at 6.45 a.m. Ugomma and Mfon stampeded into swift action of getting themselves ready before 9.30 a.m. promptly to move into the mini stadium where other freshers, their invited parents, and other relations were converging from all nooks and cranny of the town. The older students had not been left out since the entire community of the university was involved. The celebrants actually were adorned in their very best, exchanging pleasantries and admiring one another.

Mfon and Ugomma got to the venue on time to locate where their parents were seated before rushing in to meet their colleagues who were seated under the canopy alphabetically according to their respective faculties. With flashing lights, cameras were clicking away at every turn. Cheers and congratulatory pleasantries rent the air; sweet smelling fragrance permeated the atmosphere. The day looked gay, signifying summer of tropical Africa. The gentlemen of the press, from the print and electronic media, especially, the state broadcasting corporation, both the television and radio stations, were adequately present. Guests were seated before the arrival of the state governor, Obong Victor Attah, who was the special guest of honour. The entire members of the university governing council were present, including the pro-chancellor, the Eleke of Egbaland. The federal government representative, Prof. Aloy Ejiogu, the director general of the National Orientation Agency, Abuja, and his team which included Messrs Emeka Egbugara, Willy Mbagwu, and Jonathan Okeke were in attendance. The forum was used as a continuation of the campaign of the national rebirth of the present democratic dispensation.

At exactly 10 a.m., the master of ceremonies for the occasion, Dr Ukpe U. Ukpe of the Political Science Department, announced the commencement of the proceedings. The parish priest of St Peter's Catholic Church, Rev. Father Dr J. Udoh, was asked to commit the day into the care and guidance of the Supreme Living God of the Universe, after which the national anthem rent the air. That done, the band continued with marching music, which ushered in the principal authorities of the university in hierarchical order and then followed the matriculating students. After all and sundry were comfortably seated, the VC Prof. Fola Lasisi presented his welcome address. So did also the governor of Akwa Ibom State, who promised to build more hostels for the students and to provide necessary infrastructure to make life meaningful and demanded that the students should show appreciation by eschewing social vices in all facets, especially, cultism and examination malpractices.

After that, Prof. Alloy Ejiogu mounted the podium and presented his address, calling on the youths of the nation to take up the challenge of forging the course of national integration identity and spreading the symphony of brotherhood in the country in the spirit of the campaign of the national rebirth of the new democratisation. He charged them to maximally actualise this opportunity of acquiring higher education to better the lots of their families, the nation, and the entire humanity.

The VC, Prof. Fola Lasisi, after his address, observing all paraphernalia of protocols, demanded the freshers to stand up, and the oath of allegiance was administered to them. The occasion formally came to an end about 2.15 p.m. with the prayers by the officiating priest. As expected, the students availed themselves of the opportunity of snapping pictures and entertaining their invited guests.

While the university authorities proceeded to Akwa Ibom's magnificent hall at IBB Bour Louvie, off Aka Road, for a grand matriculation party, as per the culture of the institution, the UniUyo alumni association met at the Elite hotel on Udoh Umannah Road to mark the day. The Tuskers (UniUyo Alumni), along with their national president, Mr I. O. Idemeko, and other national executives, met to deliberate on vital issues concerning the progress made so far and the problems of the institution and to proffer possible solutions, with the view of communicating the same to the authorities. Also, situational reports of the local chapters for the year were reviewed.

'Ugomma, congratulations!' chorused her parents, whom she had rejoined by now.

'Thank you, Dad and Mum. I appreciate your presence here?

'Look, over there are Mr and Mrs Ekong. Where is your friend, Mfon?' her mother asked.

'She will join us after easing herself in the restroom Ugomma answered.

'Dad, let's take some photographs before the Ekongs join us Ugomma suggested.

'Sure, Ugo, you are right responded her father. 'Uchendu, I hope you can efficiently use the camera.'

'Not to worry. Let me call a professional to assist in snapping it so that you will be included in the shot.' Ugomma quickly did that, and they all posed and had it before the Ekongs joined them.

'Good afternoon, Fred, how has it been?'

'Fine, Ben.' Both the families exchanged pleasantries before Mfon walked into the gathering.

'Good afternoon, everyone she greeted them.

'Yes, my dear responded her proud mother.

'Can we all take a group picture?' Ugomma asked.

'Why not?' responded Mr Ekong as he told Ntekpere, his son, to call a professional photographer.

The boy went and came with one. 'Daddy, here he is.'

'Okay, ladies and gentlemen, shall we pose with the celebrants, Mfon and Ugomma, in the photographs as a memorial to our both families' relationship?' said Mr Ekong. They obliged him.

And the photographer said, 'Cheers, get ready. There you have it.' Thereafter, Mr Ekong gave him advance fee, as well as his office address for the delivery.

'Thank you, sir. I will surely deliver them tomorrow afternoon.' He took his leave, seeking other prospects because days like this seldom came.

'Well and good, dear Ben, the purpose of our visit has been actualised. I and my family must have to return to Lagos this evening.'

'That's all right, Fred. Let's get home, good people,' said Ben as they all moved towards the parking lot.

On the way, they were accosted by another family friend, Architect and Mrs U. S. Ekanem. 'Hello, Engr. and Mrs Ekong, how has been the day? These are your guests?'

'Yes, please meet my good friend and fellow Akokite, Mr Fred Uboma, his wife, and son. They came in from Lagos yesterday for their daughter's matriculation ceremony.'

'That's wonderful. Happy meeting you all, sir.'

'Thank you, Mr and Mrs Ekanem,' chorused the Ubomas. After this, they all drove to Ewet Housing Estate.

After a brief party and exchange of gifts, the Ubomas decided to leave for Lagos via Calabar airport. 'Dear Ben, you and your family have been a wonderful host since these two days, and I must thank you indeed,' said Mr Uboma.

'You are most welcome,' said Ben and his wife together. Their sons helped pack their luggage into the boot of the Benz car, as the Ekongs, Ubomas, and their daughters stepped outside the living room to the car.

'Goodbye, my lovely daughters,' said Mr Uboma to both Ugomma and Mfon.

They both responded, 'Goodbye, Daddy and Mummy.' Ugomma was almost shedding tears as she stood by her mother's side, holding her hands. Uchendu watched helplessly.

But her father called out, 'Hey, women, save our time. If we don't get going now, we might miss our flight.' Mrs Uboma consoled her daughter by reminding her that Christmas was just a couple of weeks away and the family would be expecting her back in Lagos.

Briskly, the Ubomas moved into the back seat of the car with Uchendu, who was waving profusely at Ugomma, his sister, while Mr Ekong sitting behind the wheels and his wife, Ufan, by his side started the car. Ntekpere opened the gate, and the car zoomed off, with Ugomma calling out to both her parents goodbye.

Thereafter, Mfon and Ugomma walked back into the house, crying. Mfon was trying her best to console and cheer up her friend, about whom she had not known or understood till that very moment how strongly attached she was to her beloved mother. 'Well, Ugomma, I understand how you feel. Please try to cheer up and remember that we have a party with our room-mates this evening. And it's about time we got ready and went back to the campus. Therefore, don't remain downcast and spoil the fine day we all had this afternoon. After all, school is gonna close in the next three weeks and you will be returning back to Lagos.' With these soothing words, Ugomma cleaned her wet eyes with the handkerchief Mfon offered her. She straightened up, beaming, and hugged her friend, then both rushed into the bathroom and showered together. They got dressed, ready to go back to the campus just as the Ekongs came back from dropping off Ugomma's parents and brother.

They arrived and Ntekpere opened the gate for them. 'Where's Ugomma?' Mrs Ekong asked. Ntekpere replied that the girls were in Mfon's room. 'Call her she ordered. While sharing gossip together, Ntekpere knocked at the door, Mfon realised that her parents were back, and they both ran downstairs to meet them in the sitting room.

'Welcome, Daddy and Mummy,' chorused both girls who were looking smashingly beautiful in their new dresses and carrying their bags gracefully as successful female bank executives. Mr and Mrs Ekong were astonished on how fast those young women had grown up in this short time. Their transformation was quite remarkable.

'Ugomma, I do understand how deeply attached you are to your lovely mother. In spite of all that care, even as the only daughter, a time comes when you must be on your own. After all, you have been doing well around here, since you came down from Lagos. Nevertheless, I must say that I appreciate your easy and fast resolve to happiness. I thought we will come back and meet you still sobbing. 'I'm all right. Thanks for caring,' responded Ugomma.

'Your power to resolve is quite commendable, Ugomma. Such quality is rare among young people of your age,' interjected Mr Ekong.

'Thank you, sir,' she replied.

'Well, Daddy, we are ready to go back to the hostel, because our roommates should be expecting us about now for a get-together said Mfon. 'Okay, my daughters, but do everything with moderation?

'Thank you for everything chorused the duo. 'Goodnight, Mummy and Daddy. Ntekpere, see you tomorrow evening?

'Bye, Sisters? They took their leave.

Getting to the hostel around 8.15 p.m., they found that they were the only members of the room absent. And now that they were back, looking gorgeously beautiful, their friends—Fatima, Yetunde, Dora—as well as other friends in the room were excited. The party commenced immediately their boyfriends started arriving. In all the hostels, various musical tunes could be heard. Parties went on unabated all around the campus. At that moment, Tony and Emeka walked into Ugomma's room and were cheerfully received by Ugomma and Mfon. After their introduction to all around, food and drinks were shared out satisfactorily. Then dancing was announced by Yetunde's boyfriend, Bayo, who had been coordinating the party earlier. He called on Ugomma and Tony to open the floor, citing William Shakespeare, 'The man who has no music in himself nor moved by the sweetness of concord of the sound, is fit for strategies and spoils. His heart is as dark as night and his mind as dark as Erebus, let not such a man be trusted.' There were lots of cheers from the audience because of Ugomma and Tony's beautiful dance steps.

'Ugomma, I didn't know that you are such a fantastic dancer whispered Tony.

'You aren't doing badly Ugomma responded. The rest of the couples joined them on the dancing floor till about 9.30 p.m. when the party ended; then chatting and clinging to his her partner, the guys left with their babes. Likewise Tony, Emeka, Ugomma, and Mfon left the room.

All that evening while the party lasted, Emeka had wrapped up a relationship with Mfon, which Tony made so happy. Now outside in the love garden, beside the business faculty building, they sat down, each couple separate from the other. 'Ugomma, do you know I'm already in love with you?' Tony asked.

'Yes, but I can't trust you that far. Meanwhile, I'm sorry about that replied Ugomma.

'There's no problem. With time, you will understand me better and those doubts will evaporate into thin air said Tony.

'Okay Ugomma responded. Holding hands together, they hugged and kissed passionately for the first time. Tony was able to extract a promise of faithfulness from her while assuring her of protection and support.

'No doubt, Ugo, you're a sweet girl, and I'm captivated by your looks. Right from the first day I met you, I actually resolved in my mind never to let you go. You can therefore imagine how happy I am right now.'

'Look, Emeka and Mfon are walking towards us. Let us meet them and part for the night because it's getting late. Hi, Emeka and Mfon, how has been the evening?'

Both chorused, 'Fine.' Ugomma could not help laughing happily, stretching out her hands to Mfon, her friend. Emeka and Tony stood beside each other now and watched admiringly as the girls warmly hugged themselves. 'Well, guys,' said Ugomma, 'we are tired and should be getting back to the room. I'm feeling drowsy and my legs are becoming weak to carry my body.' And Mfon who was leaning on Ugomma agreed to to her suggestion. Tony and Emeka thanked them for everything the evening had offered and bade them good night, promising to see them tomorrow. Getting into their room, Ugomma and Mfon lay down on their beds and slept off in their clothes, just like their room-mates who were already fast asleep.

'Boy! What a great day!' exclaimed Tony. 'Emeka, do you know that Ugomma is also in love with me?'

'Look, Tony, there's something great about her. She's forthright and does not hide her feelings nor is afraid of anyone.'

'I think you're right. From our discussion, I can understand she was greatly influenced by her background and secondary school at Queens College, Lagos,' explained Tony. 'Well, Emeka, how did you fare with Mfon? She seemed so fulfilled this night.'

'Tony, my brother, I've just proposed to her.'

'You don't mean it? You an Igbo-man and she an Ibibio girl? How on earth do you think her parents will react to that?' Tony asked.

'Chill, boy! Have you forgotten that it takes two to be or fall in love? That girl is crazy about me and she did not hide it. Rather, she advised me to tread softly. By divine Providence, whatever will be must be. In fact, Tony, I feel like a bird hovering in the sky. For any man who loves is no more alone in this wide world. Race, space, not even time can stop true love from blossoming and flourishing. So God shall provide us with the enabling and ennobling environment to get married after our graduation.'

'Congratulation, Emeka. I hope to be your best man when the time comes.'

'Yes, of course, Tony.' They slept off on this happy note.

In the following weeks, the university got ready to close briefly for the Xmas holidays. Academic works had been assigned to the students who were now craving for a break as they looked forward to joining their families. The first semester exams had been deferred to January next year when school would resume.

Meanwhile, Tony and Ugomma had been getting on fine; likewise, Emeka and Mfon also exchanged regular visits. Eventually, the last week before the Xmas break came. Ugomma came to discover that Tony had other babes on campus. She felt very bad and disturbed; her attitude reflected repugnancy for him. But he kept on trying to pacify her. Emeka and Mfon also tried to mediate and reconcile them. Ugomma accepted the reconciliation two days before the vacation. That evening, Tony and Emeka visited the girls to bid them goodbye as Ugomma and Mfon would be going to Ewet Housing Estate the following morning, and Ugomma would travel the same afternoon to Lagos. The next morning 17 December, Ugomma and Mfon got to the estate with their luggage to be welcomed by the Ekongs. Later that afternoon, the Ekongs saw Ugomma off at the office of ADC Airline on Barracks Road en route to Calabar airport, where Ugomma was to board the plane back to Lagos at 3.30 p.m. Once they got to the airline office and confirmed the booking and other necessary documentations, Mr and Mrs Ekong exchanged parting pleasantries with Ugomma, sending wishes to her family. Then Mfon hugged her, and the Ekongs drove off to Eket where they are supposed to visit that evening.

Five minutes later, the passengers boarded the airline bus for Calabar. While she waited in the departure hall of the airport, Ugomma reflected on her stay at Uyo and the university those past three to four months and adjudged her actions to be fairly above the average, but she frowned at the thought of Tony. That same moment, it was announced for the passengers to proceed and board the plane for Lagos. She, like other passengers, boarded the ADC plane. The engine roared and the plane taxied on the runway and took off. She fixed her seat belt, then meditated and relaxed as the plane became airborne. She heaved a sigh of relief and said goodbye to Canaan city and Uyo till next January.

Chapter Three

Ugomma, it's so nice to see you again. When did you return back to the campus, and how did you enjoy your Xmas holidays? How about your folks? I hope they are all well.'

'Oh, my friend, Mfon, I came back yesterday and busied myself with the task of repacking, arranging, and packing my things. I had a swell time with my family, and here is Uchendu's gift for you, especially. But the bigger package is from my parents to your whole family.'

'That's wonderful, and I am thankful to you all for being so nice,' responded Mfon.

'You are most welcome, my sister, and what about your parents?' Ugomma added.

'Well, you know my grandma is ill and hospitalised at Anua General Hospital. So they have gone to visit her, with Ntekpere.'

'Oh dear, please God spare our sweet old lady, O. Mfon, you remember those interesting folk stories she entertained us with that Saturday night that we spent the weekend with her at Eket? In fact, I was thrilled by the wisdom and acts of the tortoise, the chief character of almost every African folk story. More so, I was dazzled by the sharp and mental alertness of Grandma. It was as if her mind is marooned by the moon. She seemed to hardly forget anything.'

'O dear God, please heal Mama Ekaette, in Jesus' name. Amen!' the young ladies said.

'There is something that amazes me about you, which I am yet to figure out.'

'What is it, Mfon?'

'I just can't explain it. I feel but can't pinpoint it. It is somehow difficult, but I know it. And I hope you will not be offended with my observation.'

'No, no, my friend,' answered Ugomma.

'Okay, the way you talked about Grandma and her stories was very emotional. Such passion is from a sincere heart of an artist. The way your brown eyes shine, swimming in those beautiful sockets of your oval face, the pointed nose, sharp jaws—in fact, you radiate the epitome of elegance. At times you drift into solitude, afterwards emerge with a humming tune, like a goddess emerging from the surf of the sea, relaxed and satisfied. In fact, all about you suggests a highly talented artist. So I think you are not cut out for this course—law Mfon observed.

'Em!, thank you for the candid observation. You are truly a diligent friend. You have really touched a chord of my *being*. Fact is that I want to please my father especially. I don't want to bruise his ego, for I know that he is a proud man and highly respected among his peers and members of Ikoyi Club 1938. But I think I should be at peace with my soul doing that which comes naturally to me. For there is a course everyone is born to run, if only one can find his her path.'

'One more question, Ugo, what is your zodiac sign?'

'I am an Aries. 2 April is my birthday. What about it, Mfon?'

'Nothing serious,' Mfon responded, 'but it simply explains more about your natural gifts and characteristic behaviours which are generally associated with the people of the same influential dispositions from the supra-natural.'

'That's interesting!' Ugomma exclaimed. 'Please explain further. I am all ears.'

'Yes, Aries people are not initiators of new ideas. They rely on others to lead, thereby, are vulnerable to selfish and negative-minded persons, who can easily exploit them Mfon continued.

'*Wa* O! What more do you know about things like this?' Ugomma asked.

'Well, I am a Cancerian, from 22 June to 21 July. Our general characteristic disposition is that we are simple but delicate and really decisive. We are also bearing and forbearing, an attitude which the other person may deem being soft or foolish, but would be surprised the day we react based on a long period of diligent observations and garnered information.'

'That sounds great,' remarked Ugomma.

'Personally, I love blue and white colours, which depict love and purity,' Mfon said.

'Me too, my favourite colours are brown and green,' Ugomma added.

'You see, that represents being earthy and in love with life,' explained Mfon.

'Above all, I believe in self-grooming based on personal aspiration, which ultimately makes or mars an individual. Does this zodiac thing actually work?' Ugomma queried.

'Take it or leave it. They are the transferred knowledge of the ancient, which is still relevant in the contemporary: "Facts are stubborn. They refuse to be obliterated and obscured".'

'You are right, Mfon. No knowledge is a waste. Well, so be that as it may for now.'

'Ugomma, did you come in contact with Tony during the holidays?'

'Yes, my dear, he called me twice from Onitsha. I think he also had a swell time because his cousins visited from overseas. Two arrived home from Dallas, United States of America, and the third guy from Germany. A lot of activities, jiving engaged his time.

'You know, the Igbos being the most enterprising tribe in Nigeria woke up from the ashes of that wicked civil war fought right inside their homeland to annihilate them, dust the debris of deliberate wreckages by the federal troops, rejuvenated into a boisterous renaissance of great commerce, leading to an exodus for greener pastures into the developed world of America and Europe, whereby did exist the enabling and ennobling environment fully adequate to express their natural given talents and ingenuity in all facets of education. Hence, the undying spirit of Biafara, rather the Igboman, is manifested in the maintenance and careful transfer of socio-cultural norms and values to succeeding generations. Connectively, in the heart of Igbo land is Ndibinuhu, Abu eke Community in Ihitte Uboma council area, where you have the festival of wearing of cloths (Iwa Akwa) ceremony performed once in every three years depicting maturity from boyhood to manhood, who can now sit in the elders council to deliberate and contribute to issues of importance and also become taxable adults. There is also the clearing of road (Igbo Uzo) ceremony performed annually in December before Christmas. These festivals are peculiar to the communities within the Okigwe senatorial zone of Imo State.

'Also in Mbaise, the kola nut (Orji) festival is performed in December period, while the "Ofala" day festival is performed in Anambra, Enugu, and

Ebonyi States, depicting homage being paid to the traditional kingdoms of Obis and Igwes. The "Mgboto nma" ceremony in some parts of Abia State depict the traditional retirement whereby the elderly, sixty-five years and above, are exonerated from local labours and levies.

'These and many more cultural heritage of the Igbos became the bedrock for fostering the resilient spirit of that renaissance which attracts sons and daughters in diasporas from all over the world during Xmas, especially when igba nkwu nwanyi (traditional marriages) are contemporarily performed across Igbo land. In all these merriments, Tony complained of missing me. Come to think of it, Mfon, do you think he is serious?' Ugomma asked.

'He could be, my sister.'

'Why?'

'Because I believe in the philosophy of change, especially if it is positive and result oriented. So I will advise you to give him a chance,' replied Mfon.

'That's okay. You don't kill a man with a mud sling. You don't need to tell me about Emeka. I know he loves you dearly.'

'You are perfectly correct, Ugo. We are together in the spirit all the time. That's how I feel for him.'

'Anyway, when are you coming back to the campus?' Ugomma asked.

'I should be back tomorrow evening around 6 p.m. You know, after church service, I will finally pack the leftover things that I would have remembered before Daddy will drive me down.'

'No problems,' Ugomma said. 'I have to go now. Regards to your parents when they return and please don't forget to hand over those packages from my parents to them. See you in the hostel tomorrow then.'

'Okay, Ugo, good night.'

Three days later, Tony and Emeka visited Ugomma and Mfon. The hostels were still empty because students were still carrying forward the hang-over euphoria of Xmas holidays. Really, at this time they returned in a trickle until about three weeks or one month when a full house could be expected. The ripple effect of this attitude and approach affected the entire economic ecology of the whole town, considering the fact that education was virtually the industry that sustained the business community here. But the VC, Professor F. Lasisi, bearing in mind the tight scheduled academic nature of the second semester and other curricula activities as well as focus on achieving academic excellence ordered that lectures should commence in earnest two weeks after resumption. Following this development, that fateful evening was a well-articulated and opportune time, a conducive atmosphere, for early returnees to practicalise the promise of love.

'Listen, Mfon, there is a gentle tap on the door?

'Yes, who is there? Please come in,' responded Mfon. Tony and Emeka ushered themselves into the room, smiling; of course, it was a delightful reunion as the girls ran into the warm embrace of their boyfriends.

Meanwhile, since the Harmattan breeze still blew everywhere drily across the tropical vegetation, she fragrantly blew the sweet-smelling scents of the queen of night flower into the room, tantalising the libido of a perfect romantic setting. Still holding each other in separate beds, the couples drifted into a romantic frenzy, entangled in savouring it all, only to break free when the fire had died and was out. Then they awoke and came to consciousness of their surroundings, relaxed and smiling at each other like little innocent children in a free world. 'Ugomma, do you know that I called your home again last week and was informed by your kid brother, Uchendu, that you had left back for the campus? I guessed right that you and Mfon must have returned here, so I called Emeka and confirmed our earlier return back to campus. Now it has paid off, isn't?' Tony asked.

'Yes,' replied Emeka. 'Sweethearts, how were the Xmas holidays?'

The duo chorused heartily, 'Fine.'

'You know, ladies and gentleman, there is going to be lots of socio-political activities in the campus this second semester. Usually, second semester is shorter in duration, yet cumbered with serious academic works, students' union week-long activities, including "ragging", whereby students deliberately wear tattered cloths and with containers bearing caption of "donate to charity" move from place to place in the towns and cities, urging people to put money into the container. Other activities are beauty pageant contests, sports, election of new student union functionaries. In fact, the extracurricular activities will galvanise the entire system. Therefore, we must not lose focus on our primary objective which is academics,' Tony advised.

'Who are the possible candidates for the students' union election for now?' Emeka asked.

'There is a guy Stanley from the Communication Arts Department. I learnt he is hot academically with a good GPA of over four points, in fact, he is a First Class material. And there is another guy from Accounting Department, an Ibibio extraction. Emeka, you know as I do, that the number of candidates for the presidency will certainly increase as the time progresses.'

'Men! Why don't you give this political yarn a hiatus for now? You politicians like trading your stuffs at every given opportunity,' said Mfon.

'No, darling, please be well informed that we are not politicians but political scientists, exploring the frontier of knowledge with the view of postulating and professing solutions to social problems of statehood, governance, and proper management of administration of resources. We provide basically the enabling and ennobling environment for man to explore, improve, and contribute and enjoy also the fruit of his labour. The foregoing is the borderline between us and the so-called politicians who are selfish, greedy, power mongers without principles and fortitude towards their fellow citizens.'

'Mfon, he is right agreed Ugomma.

Tony started another topic. 'Ugomma, I have something important to ask of you in the presence of our friends here?

'Yes, what is it?' she responded. Emeka and Mfon listened with great attention, although Emeka was already aware of the bombshell.

'Ugo, will you marry me?' Tony asked. Ugomma was taken aback and momentarily dumb founded, because she thought Tony had been previously joking. She regarded the relationship as a mere casual friendship that would either grow or fizzle out like a passing impulse with time. But reality is powerful and comes with a force that if not prepared can destabilise one on the first value. When she eventually found her voice, it sounded strange and rattled, but her quick power to resolve situations surprised Tony and Emeka, who were encountering her for the first time in such a mood. Mfon had an immediate flashback of the time when Ugomma's parents departed back for Lagos after their matriculation last semester.

Rather, Ugomma diplomatically asked Tony, 'Sebi, that's a futuristic proposal that can start now, isn't it?' Tony answered by nodding his head, looking straight into Ugomma's eyes. 'Well, I've come to like and accept you as a friend, but marriage must have to wait,' she answered.

'But look, Ugomma, even Emeka and Mfon have consented to each other said Tony.

'That shows that they are right individuals in a free world. I'm myself and not competing with anybody. For I know that there's no competition in destiny, no matter the view or action of another person. After all, what matters most is to know yourself and your ways, and what you often think about yourself.'

'Tony, please let this issue rest for now,' interjected Mfon. 'I'll talk to my friend later about it.'

'Okay, that's a great idea, Tony. It has gone well into the night, and let's give these babes a break for tonight and see them tomorrow evening,' reasoned Emeka.

'Oh, yeah,' replied Tony, still not happy.

'Look, Tony, don't feel bad about it, but please try to understand.'

'Okay, Ugomma,' he responded. And they all stepped outside. As they saw them off, Ugomma walked beside Tony, and Emeka passionately held hands with Mfon. The babes unanimously stopped at the exit gate of the annex campus and exchanged good night kisses with their boyfriends and returned back to their room.

In the next couple of weeks, full academic activities resumed in the entire campus. In one of Ugomma's new law courses, she encountered a don called Dr Alexander Ogubuike Egbugara, who dazzled them with the most eloquent views she had ever heard. The lecturer, unlike other days, entered the class that morning like a man walking on the pedestal of vision propelled by the zeal to inform the youths about the will of the Sovereign Lord of the universe. The preamble he introduced captivated the interest of the entire class, enthralling them in rapt attention. 'Men of diadem are those who live to contribute positively towards the development and benefit of humanity.'

'Mfon! Did you hear that?' Ugomma said.

The don continued, 'Life and living is all about relationship with God and service to humanity. But man is at his best serving others. This is the sacrifice, the supreme sacrifice to love that the entire universe evolves and depends upon.' He referred to President John F. Kennedy's speech to the United States of America's Congress on 28 February 1963: 'Our Nation is founded on the principle that observance of the Law is the eternal safeguard of Liberty, andany act of defiance from this, is the surest road to anarchy... Even among law-abiding men, few laws are universally loved but others are universally respected and not resisted. Men are free to disagree with the law, because no man, however prominent or powerful and no mob however unruly or boisterous is entitled to defy the law.'

The don also referred to the seven deadly sins as postulated by Mahatma Gandhi of India: (1) wealth without work, (2) knowledge without character (better balance between the development of character and intellect), (3) pleasure without conscience or lack of sense of responsibilities, (4) commerce (business) without morality (ethic), (5) science without humanity, (6) religion without service (seeking for the benefits of others), (7) politics without principle.

The lecturer went further to emphasise, 'There's a labyrinth so thin but with a plain surface on which atoms run at the fastest speed ever known, even faster than the speed of light-thoughts in the human man. Mind is the nucleus of all activism, positive and negatives, depending on the individual's inclination, ability, and matured disposition. Above all, the real essence lies in objectivism which is the framework that should propagate to eternity. This is because goodness is never lost in time, but blooms into eternity bliss. Hence, if I can recommend, people who should be admitted to read law in our universities are only those born with aflame spirit and vision only to defend the course of justice against injustice. Use the power of law and annihilate man's inhumanity to man. Give hope and succour to the downtrodden who run into their courts as a last resort for liberty from the subjugation strangulation of the arrogant mighty and lofty men of vain societies. And not the pompous and frivolous siblings of the perpetuators of subjugations who see or regard the law profession as an appendix of family name and do not realise that as a misnomer to societal values and norms. Let such frivolous elements learn or study law, but should be forever banned from entering the courtrooms or from presiding or determining the affairs of other men, for that is murder. But let my radical learned gentlemen advance the course of rebirth, for they are the light that shines in darkness and reflects brightness around their environment. And so be they remembered. Ladies and gentlemen, let's call it a day.'

With the lecture over then, Mfon and Ugomma went back to their hostel to rest awhile before going for lunch at their usual spot at Udoette. That evening, there was a notice of meeting by the Federation of Igbo students at the pavilion in the main campus. Tony and Emeka came to call on Ugomma and other female Igbo students, who were reluctant in attending such ethnic-based political meetings that had engulfed the other tribal inclinations like the National Association of Akwa Ibom State Students, the Oduduwa Association. Midnight caucus meetings were being held across the campuses. 'There are merger formations going on in this campus, which have intensified their activities, recently called "kparakpo" groupings,' said Emeka.

'That sounds interesting, but I don't have the time to spare for such gatherings, so count me out please,' said Ugomma. Tony was surprised by such utterance, but was content with it; he knew that people with such mental attitude or disposition realised their folly when the chips of arrogance and ignorance were down.

'Only let it not be too late for Ugomma,' he wished. Therefore, he left with Emeka for the venue of the meeting, feeling disappointed.

The student union week came to a climax on the manifesto night, and it attracted lots of students to the pavilion, which was filled to its capacity. Each of the nine presidential candidates was to mount the podium and make their speeches. Stanley started thus, 'Ladies and gentlemen, all protocols duly observed, let us all synchronise the symphony of national brotherhood, eschew parochial tribal sentiments and inclinations that have bedevilled this nation for wasted decades. These evils are locusts which have plundered our green vegetations, dried and desolate. Men and brethren, let's extend the hand of fellowship across the Niger, stretched from the basin of the Atlantic in the south to the sparse Savannah regions of the north. That our great natural and human resources do not lie in the doldrums perpetually, for history shall never be kind or merciful to memories of the bad leaders who selfishly and greedily squander the wealth and pride of this nation when the annals therefore are reviewed in posterity. This university is therefore a micro-system that represents Nigeria at large. The vision I have sincerely posed I hope to actualise if you give me the mandate, so help me God?

There was a thunderous ovation which trailed Stanley to his seat, depicting acceptance by a large number of the non-indigenes who collectively resolved to rewrite the history of the institution as far as the presidency of the student union government was concerned. Consequent to this development, the other candidates from Akwa Ibom State announced their stepping down so that Etim became the only indigeneous candidate. So the contest was drawn between Stanley, representing the interest of all the non-indigenes, and him.

The frenzy of this election was so high and intense that the mafia groups were seen carrying firearms openly. Even the local paramount rulers become partisan and vocally declared such an elated position as their birthright. All said and done, the election was rigged and won by the indigenes. Since the result almost tore the university into shreds, the VC invited security operatives from the State Police Command to forestall the envisaged chaos. However, the students resolved to let sleeping dogs lie, bearing in mind the very purpose that had brought them there.

'Ugomma, what are the things left out in the preparation for your birthday in the next two days?' Mfon asked.

'I think everything has been taken care of. That means there would not be any hitches to a successful party?

'But let's be sure and run through the entire arrangements once again, because there's no fortress without an underbelly, according to Hadley Chase,' suggested Mfon. She obliged, and they were satisfied.

Sunday, 2 April, time 5 p.m.: Venue was the Sky-view Hotel, main hall, last floor, Barracks Road, Uyo. The birthday party for Ugomma had just begun, and her guests were already seated, chatting hilariously. Amongst them were her room-mates—Fatima, Yetunde, Dora—and other friends and their boyfriends. The hall was filled to capacity because Ugomma during this period in her university career had become popular, especially within the annex campus. A lot of guys even referred to her as the yet-to-be crowned Miss UniUyo. They obviously were falling heads over heels to catch her fancy, but Ugomma was not for all comers. It was no wonder that the information about this party had passed round a week previously. America valued information a great deal and vouched to rule the world with it. That's just the lot of the university communities where students traded for it.

Conversely, babes could not help but be jealous of Ugomma, who seemed to have everything going well for her. She was from a rich home and just celebrating her seventeenth birthday, elegantly standing at 1.92 metres, gracefully beautiful, fair, and adorned with rich flowing hair that superbly and graciously settle on her shoulder. Her dazzling swimming brown eyes were her greatest asset. This evening on this occasion, a guy called Junior from the Communication Arts Department was the MC, a smooth and fast-talking guy with the Warri-Port Harcourt accent. The vibes from the loudspeakers were too strong to be resisted by the lovers of good music. The hotel management operated a catering outfit, so Ugomma availed herself of their services instead of bothering with cooking and drinks. Hence, there was enough food and drinks, even to spare. 'Ladies and gentlemen, while the music of Jim Reeves is playing the track 'Across the bridge there's no more sorrow the sun will shine, and you will never be unhappy again', shall we all arise and herald the arrival of the celebrant and her entourage, Ugomma Uboma? Here we are, good folks. Cheer and welcome this epitome of beauty, simply referred to as the yet to-be crowned Miss UniUyo. She is indeed a pride to this institution the MC announced. Ugomma was now comfortably seated beside Tony while Mfon and Emeka sat next to them. And there was this sense of fulfilment and joy radiating around Ugomma, which seemed contagious as she beamed, showing dimples on her rosy cheeks and sparkling white teeth.

She was dressed in a maroon-coloured gown with its collar adorned with diamond stones plus a necklace, an expensive wristwatch, a black hat, handbag, and shoes to match, which her mother had bought for her on her trip to London a month before. The combination produced a wonderful effect, and the transformation had kept Tony and Emeka transfixed in bewilderment the moment they stepped into Ugomma's room, before arriving at the party venue.

And now they could understand how Ugomma felt inside as she drew up a smile that was wrecking the feelings of other men in that forum. Besides, Mfon who knew Ugomma's mother well was not perplexed about this smiling goddess seated next to her spick and span, smelling ostentatiously sweet because of the designer perfume she was wearing. At this juncture, ladies and gentlemen declared the MC, 'may I have the pleasure to call upon the celebrant, Ms Ugomma Uboma, to formally declare this party open by the way of an address? On your honour, please, Ugomma.' The voice of Ugomma was like the whispering breeze at the seashore, which the microphone transformed into a gentle echo till the end of the hall. Tony, her boyfriend, could not believe his ears, even Emeka, but not Mfon. The gathering that was hearing her for the first time, besides her roommates that were present, talked less.

The speech was precise but concise. Her speech centred on the essence of ambition and actualisation of destiny. The audience gave her a standing ovation, after which she blew out the candles on her cake. And they sang the happy birthday chorus for her, preceding the cutting of her cake.

To open the dancing floor, Tony requested a blues; hence, the DJ slotted on a track from Godsmind's LP 'Love is the ocean'. And it was like a give-it-all-to-me warm embrace while it lasted for Tony. Nothing good lasts forever here on earth, as the track played off and the MC invited the guests to the dancing floor, quoting William Shakespeare, 'If music be the food of love play on'. The video camera man and photographer were also doing their things, in whichever segments. Food and drinks were also served around.

'Ugomma, you are a star, any day, any time,' complimented Tony.

'Oh, thanks for appreciating me.'

'Let's go out to the balcony,' said Tony, while the party went on.

While there, Tony said to Ugomma, 'You know I can't stop loving you. Why not marry me?'

'Look, Tony, time is the most determinant factor in the entire world. Give me more time to think about your proposal. I will surely tell you my mind someday. Moreover, exams shall soon start in a couple of weeks from now, then the long vacation preceding your final year and the second year for me. I think then it should be appropriate to finalise this important issue. Meanwhile, Tony, you've been so nice this evening. I feel strengthened and supported by you making me feel cherished and appreciated. I will forever remember that.' Tony's action replied for him, as he instantaneously drew her into his arms and passionately kissed her. Holding hands together, they walked back into the dancing hall.

'It has been a fulfilled and wonderful evening, ladies and gentlemen,' declared the MC. 'Getting into the wee-nigh hours of the dawning day, I suppose the party should be ending about now but not without the celebrant giving her vote of thanks.'

'Tony, please stand in for me. I'm so tired,' pleaded Ugomma. Hence, Tony stepped forward and took over the mike from the MC.

'We thank all of you for jettisoning your personal programmes to honour and stay out this invitation. We appreciate the gesture because to love and share is good nature, and to appreciate no matter how great or small a kindness is a gesture that fosters good friendliness and better human understanding. Welcome and so long.' That was his final note. Finally, the party was dispatched in a Toyota bus hired by Ugomma to convey everyone back to the campus. Thereafter, Tony, Emeka, Mfon, and herself got to the annex campus in a cab which dropped them at the entrance gate, and the driver sped off.

Sitting down on the pavement in front of a kiosk, they evaluated the party and concluded that it had been a successful outing. Indeed, tired and sleepy, both the couples kissed each other good night, and the babes approached the entrance of their hostel, while the duo of Tony and Emeka returned to their room.

In the next couple of weeks, Ugomma's successful birthday party was the talk of the campus, as the university community got ready for the second semester exams and subsequent long vacation. The final year students were tidying up their project works. Tony and Emeka, the prospective finalists, had been assigned as supervisory lecturers and project topics had been approved for them. The general student body was itching to go back home to their families, especially those from poor backgrounds, who had almost exhausted their financial resources and was only managing to survive on 0-0-1 or 1-0-1 feeding ratio. In fact, it was the most precarious time in the life of a student as an undergraduate in the Nigerian university system.

'Mfon, the time table for the exams was published on the departmental notice board this afternoon. The part two and above students will round up their exams two weeks before us?

'But that is not fair Mfon responded.

'You remember what happened last semester? After their exams, the male students stayed back and disturbed the others with incessant toasting and invading the female hostels. It was even alleged that some female students going and returning back from classes late in the night were raped?

'Ugomma, I think it's proper that the university authorities should slot the exam to commence and end simultaneously to avoid a reoccurrence of such ugly incident? responded Mfon.

'Worst still! observed Ugomma, 'is the unreliable power outage by PHCN. They are a menace. Imagine students going to the classrooms with candlelights, lanterns, chargeable lamps, and what not. The entire scene looked like Oshodi night market?

'Look, Ugomma, I didn't find it funny last semester concerning this issue, but let's hope for a better situation this time around since the generators have been fixed.'

'Let's hope so,' replied Ugomma. 'We should go in for dinner immediately so that we can rest awhile before going to class.'

'That's all right by me,' responded Mfon.

'Emeka, when is the "state and economy" paper coming up?' Tony asked.

'Tomorrow from 9.30 a.m. to 11.30 a.m.,' replied Emeka.

'Okay, thanks,' responded Tony.

On the morrow, at about 11.25 a.m., gunshots could be heard from the annex campus; students ran helter-skelter, cries and shouts of woes reaching the main campus where exams were still in progress. 'Emeka, what's going on?' Tony asked, as they both came out of the examination hall.

'The bad boys, cult mafias, of course, are at it again. This time around it seems the worst bloody,' responded Emeka.

'But why always during exam period?'

'It is a simple logic. They don't sit down to read as they indulge in constant clandestine activities from one university campus to another around the country and beyond, intimidating other students and lecturers, especially the female students whom they coerce into affairs. By and large, the contention is for supremacy among various mafia groups as the dominant entity within the campus. And within two days, more than twenty dead bodies were picked from locations within the campus. The worst spot was the Ravin area. What a Hollywood display in a citadel of higher learning! Tony, do you know that just this morning BBC reported the incident and referred UniUyo as the most notorious institution of higher learning in Africa?'

'That means taking off the shine of notoriety from the University of Calabar,' responded Tony.

'Yes O,' said Emeka. 'Come to think of it, UniUyo for years has been producing high-quality graduates in all disciplines, even as the best at the Nigerian Law School three years consecutively now. And this recent scandalous incident, where do we go from here?' Emeka asked.

'Remember the parable of the tare? Our Lord Jesus Christ said that a farmer went out and sowed good seeds, but at night, the enemy went and contaminated them by planting his bad seeds. And as they grew up in the nursery stage together, the labourers sought the Farmer's permission to weed them away, but he advised them to leave them to grow together till the harvest time Tony replied.

'That reminds me of the story I heard about one Papa J in the business faculty. He was a kingpin of one of the mafia groups and spent eight years on this campus as an undergraduate pursuing one degree course. He actually was stunned beyond measure when his course mate from year one came around with a very beautiful car. It dawned on him the fool he has made of himself and years wasted chasing shadows. Do you know that that was the turning point in his life? He repented and became an apostle of positive change, advising others to forget cultism and trust God for their very essence that brought them to school. It is no gainsay that these gangsters are influenced right from their family background, where they have observed their parents belong to one secret cult or another. So what do you expect?'

'They are just chips of the old blocks agreed Emeka. 'With this step to a new life, as lots of them across the nation's universities were denouncing cultism, the lecturers had pity on Papa J and let him go with a pass-out from the system.'

'Lucky him responded Tony. 'Imagine those who died and wasted in the process, those maimed for life and dropouts. Oh! Countless woes and lost hopes to the families, the psychological trauma for the raped victims all through life. This is a crazy world he concluded.

Look, my brother, Tony, it is as if humanity in the twenty- first century is drifting back to the state of nature where injustice, brutality, and wickedness excelled without regard to the tenet of the Rule of Law (sovereign and national laws). I think it is the worst in Africa observed Emeka.

'Methinks the black man in this last millennium is a man tired of living and still afraid to die responded Tony.

'You may be right, boy, depending on the perspective from which you look at it concluded Emeka.

'Well, Tony, congratulations. We are now through with the exams'Thanks, same to you, my brother, Emeka. I am sick of this environment and would want to leave tomorrow morning if not for Ugomma whom I must see before departing said Tony.

'You are right, my friend. I also need to see my heartthrob, Mfon, and encourage her for her forthcoming exams responded Emeka. 'Let's go and see them

The next day, 27 July, at 5 p.m., the duo went to see their friends, Ugomma and Mfon. 'Yes, who is there? Do come in responded Ugomma to the knock at the door. Then Tony and Emeka entered into the room. 'Good evening, gentlemen greeted Ugomma.

'Good evening, Ugomma chorused the duo.

'How has it been with your exams?'

'Very well, it's all over now, ushering us into the final year they responded.

'Where is Mfon?' Emeka asked.

'Oh, she is taking her bath.'

Five minutes later, Mfon entered the room looking fresh and sweet. 'Hi, gentlemen, and congratulations. I believe that you had no problems in rounding up your exams?'

'Oh darling, all that matters now is the enthusiasm of starting our project work in earnest, especially during this long vacation. More so, I and Tony have decided to depart from this town first thing tomorrow to PH city enroute Aba, the Enyimba city.'

'Yes, I understand you guys came this evening to bid us farewell, isn't it?' Mfon asked.

'You are right, sweetheart responded Tony. 'In fact, we are gonna share dinner this evening, a special treat I and Emeka have planned for us all, but the honour is yours to pick the spot.'

'That's great. Mfon, shut that door please. Let's dress up said Ugomma.

'That's okay by me too, Ugo. This evening is not meant for that Udoette stuff. Our great guys are giving us a treat to wind up the semester, so let's make it special for them to compliment them,' said Mfon while they dressed up in the extreme corner of the room. 'What dress are you choosing for the outing?'

'That black evening wear that my auntie sent to me from USA last semester,' answered Ugomma.

'I remember it. It fits you.'

'I know Emeka will be all over you this evening. That's the way guys boast their ego and care.'

'No two ways about it, Ugomma. I am deeply in love with my fiance, Emeka,' responded Mfon. After finishing getting dressed, they both walked into the arms of their boyfriends.

'Mfon, I bless the day I found you, and it has remained indelible in my mind, and every other passing day and moments together, like now, reassures me that there is no mistake about finding you. Your bulging sexy eyes are electrifying. The current vibrates down my spine. I can't just resist you, my darling,' Emeka complimented Mfon.

'I am happy. You also know that I sincerely love you, Emmy, and promise to remain yours faithfully. I know and understand you. I'm going to make you happy forever, trust me.'

'Okay, Mfon baby, I have trusted you before now,' responded Emeka.

'Ugo, my princess, you look like Diana of Great Britain, that lovely lady who gave her love estate to the man who would have been hers, away from the probing eyes of passers-by who flaunt the moments of others' quiet private life.'

'Look, Tony, stop flattering me.'

'Yes, darling, more than flattering is the truth, and that I won't hide from you. You look rejuvenated every moment with the expressive mind of a poet, as if you have drunk straight from the fountain of living waters.'

'No doubt, Tony, I am in love with life,' responded Ugomma. 'That's why I resolve quickly to peace and happiness within, no matter the situation prevailing. It's a tonic and preserver of good health.'

'Time to go, good people,' announced Emeka.

'Oh yeah, shall we go?' chorused the others. And all together they strolled out of the room and outside; as they walking towards the annex gate, they stopped a cab and headed towards the central town.

Eureka Peace Restaurant was the happening place in town which the oil boys of Mobil patronised with their female undergraduate babes for cosy times.

'Here we are, folks. Feel comfortable and enjoy yourselves said Tony. Harold Steward's song 'Sweet evening for sweetheart that shall never end' was filtering in from a loudspeaker concealed somewhere in the room. The place was not crowded except for the chosen few that appreciated the value for their money. Decency and friendliness was the decorum of the place, a place for matured minds to relax and reappraise life. No wonder the big boys from Mobil Oil Company flocked there as their exclusive spot.

They placed their orders with the smart-looking youthful waiters dressed in white and black suits. The security guards patrolled round the place. At the tarmac heading to the swimming pool were beautiful portal flowers of various blended colours. Segments of tables and chairs were arranged to accommodate couples in four, six, two formations. The gentle breeze that blew spread round the sweet fragrance of the queen of the night flower, as if nature knew nothing but giving and sharing love to all creatures.

When their dinner was over, Tony paid up the bill, and they stepped outside, satisfied, crushing the granite as they moved towards the exit gate. Tony called out to Ugomma, 'This is a never-forget-me place. Their services are superb and decent. No wonder the penultimate weekend, my room-mates were gisting about it. How a customer came to the room next door and invited all the babes there where the oil boys were organising a social function. The babes came back with lots of doles and juicy gists?

'What do you mean by a customer?' Ugomma asked. 'Is it a nonfellow male student who comes around to the hostels looking for babes?'

'Oh yeah, they are suppressors,' responded Tony.

'Mfon, are you all right?' Emeka asked.

'Perfectly well,' she responded.

'Tony, let's make a stopover at the convocation park before taking these babes back to their hostel later,' suggested Emeka.

'How about that, Ugomma? Why don't we relax in the love garden beside the business block at the annex campus since it is close to our hostel so that even if it is late we can still make it without hindrance?'

'It's better,' agreed Mfon. Hence, their cab pulled up at the annex gate. Ugomma paid off the driver, and they turned and walked towards the garden.

'Hi, jolly folks greeted Yetunde, who was with her boyfriend, Bayo.

'Hello, Yetunde replied Ugomma. 'How was the evening?'

'Fine responded Yetunde and her friend. 'So long and see you later.'

'Tony, do you know that at times I come out here alone when I want to meditate in absolute solitude?' said Ugomma.

'How do you mean?'

'When there is much compelling stress due to academic works, I come out here only to be at peace. One on one with nature like this in the night with the feel of the gentle breeze blowing cuddles my soul and fills my breath with fragrance of the queen of the night flower. Can't you hear the whispering trees in consonance like the tune from a piano?' Ugomma asked.

'Yes, my princess, but not with that kind of deeper feelings, almost rhapsodic. Otherwise, one operates from the frequency that he knows and belongs to.'

While they relaxed in each other's warm embrace, Mfon and Emeka sitting a little away from them were lost in wild romance; as Ugomma heard the soft moaning of her friend in ecstasy, she smiled knowingly; it was as if in response to the comment made by Tony beside her.

'Tony, please take it easy. Your exploring hands are wrecking my sensuality,' she pleaded. Tony breathed a sigh of exhaustion and planted a deep kiss on the pomegranate mouth of Ugomma, just as Emeka and Mfon stood up and walked towards them.

'Shall we go?' Emeka enquired, holding hands with Mfon.

'Why not?' Tony responded, as they all walked back to the front of Wl. 'Ugomma, have a nice stay in these remaining couple of weeks and ensure that you do in your exams, okay?'

'Thanks, Tony, do keep in touch?

'And you, Mfon, best of luck in your exams?

'Thank you, Tony,' responded Mfon.

'Good night, my sweetheart. I'll keep in contact,' Emeka addressed Mfon. 'So long, Ugomma?

'Goodbye, Emeka? The babes walked into the common room of their hostel, while Tony and Emeka walked away—into the next academic year.

Chapter Four

After the exams, Ugomma travelled back to Lagos on 19 August. While she was there at the ADC airline terminus on Barracks Road, waiting for the bus to ferry the passengers to Calabar airport, where they would board the flight to Lagos, Steven Daniel, a cool-looking, calculating guy working in Mobil QIT started chatting her up. Before arriving at Calabar that afternoon, the duo had gotten quite familiar and exchanged addresses; the guy gave his complimentary card with his home contact number at Eket, as Ugomma couldn't precisely say where her hostel accommodation would be until the next academic year began the second week of October. Therefore, the onus rested with her to contact Daniel when she resumed and settled down in her new hostel.

They had a smooth flight to Lagos, exchanged pleasantries, and parted to go their different ways. Ugomma's folks were at the airport to receive her home. Her mother, elder brother Chimebuka, and Uchendu were waiting in the arrival hall, when the ADC flight arrived and the passengers queued up to collect their luggage. Ugomma caught sight of her elder brother, whom she had not seen for a long while, and they hugged each other. The transformation in Ugomma was quite remarkable in all facets of life so that her elder brother, Chimebuka, commented immediately while they were riding home. 'Mother, I missed you all. Why is Daddy not here with you people?' Ugomma asked.

'Your father travelled overseas, precisely Indonesia, on a business trip and is expected back in a week's time,' responded her mother.

'Chime, I suppose you came back home last week as indicated in the message you passed through Mrs G. Ebong, the manager at the NITEL territorial office in Uyo.'

'Yes, Ugo, we finished exams two weeks previously, so I came back here before Daddy travelled.'

'Hi, Uchendu, how are your school and studies? I hope you are doing well.'

'Yes, Sister Ugomma, things are perfectly all right, except that I missed you dearly.'

'Not to worry, my dear. I'm home for two months' long vacation. I hope you received the card which I mailed to you last month?'

'Yes, Sister Ugo, I'm grateful. Thanks a lot,' responded Uchendu.

'How is Maraako? Why did he not come to the airport?'

'He went for lessons,' her mother explained.

Her elder brother continued, 'Ugomma, you have really changed tremendously beyond my grand expectations. You are handsomely more beautiful, like a blossoming rose flower, sounding greatly polished with an acquired lady-like attitude.'

'Thanks, Ebuka,' she responded. 'You know, once in the system, one has to imbibe the university enculturation. And there is no way you pass through a system and allow the system also to do the same to you without noticeably getting affected positively and objectively.'

'You are right, my sister.'

Listening to the discussion of her undergraduate children, who had suddenly become young adults, stirred up a lot of joy in Mrs Ihuoma Uboma's heart. In particular, it was remarkable that Ugomma, her only daughter, had grown up into a smashing beautiful young woman, addressing her as Mother and not as Mummy as she used to do. Mrs Uboma had actually noticed the young man who arrived in that flight with Ugomma and how they exchanged pleasantries before they parted. No doubt, her daughter had started socialising with men. That she took notice of although Ugomma had never been a shy person all her life long.

Meanwhile, they got to their home at Victoria Island, and on hearing the car's horn, Sule, their security man, opened the gate and Ebuka drove the Toyota Jeep Land Cruiser in and parked in the garage, then the occupants stepped out. 'Welcome, madam,' Sule greeted.

'Thank you, Sule. Did anyone come here while I was away?'

'No, ma. *Haba*, Ugomma, you are welcome O" Sule's children, Hajiya, and Felicia, their housemaid, all rushed out to welcome Ugomma.

'Hajiya, how are you and the children?'

'We are fine,' she responded.

'Welcome back, Ugomma,' hailed Felicia, who was helping in carrying her luggage upstairs. Earlier, Felicia had tidied up Ugomma's room and changed the beddings, and the place looked decent. Even the flowers in the compound were neatly trimmed, their sparkling swimming pool blue colours alluringly inviting. And from the kitchen came the aroma of delicious cooking flavour which permeated the surroundings. Ugomma instantly felt hungry, as she remembering she had not yet had her lunch, after taking breakfast in Mfon's house.

'How are the Ekongs?' her mother enquired.

'O! Mama, they are actually doing well, and they send their regards to the whole family. Uchendu, your friend Mfon sends her regards?

'Thanks, Sister Ugo. I like sister Mfon so much. She is a nice person and she cares a lot. How is her kid brother, Ntekpere?' Uchendu asked.

'He is fine, too? After Ugomma had a bath and felt refreshed, the entire household came to the dining table with their mother at the head of the table since her husband, Igwe, had travelled out. After benediction, they settled down to eat their food; orange drinks were on the table as well. After food, her mother urged her to eat more cake, observing that she needed to gain more weight and recover fully in the next couple of days, because the exams had sapped her and made her lean.

'Ugomma, why not eat more cake? You look famished. Even your eyes seemed to have sunk inside. You must have burnt yourself through the nights without resting enough?

'O, Mama, thanks for caring this much. I am satisfied for now. I cannot take in any more food until the night. Right now, I need to catch some sleep. I am already feeling drowsy?

'Okay, my daughter, you can go upstairs to your room? Ugomma immediately left the table and walked regally up the staircase while the rest of the eyes trailed her.

'Good day, guys she greeted her brothers who had become apprehensive of this Princess Diana that their only sister had become now. Ebuka, unconsciously, right from the airport had started admiring his sister because she was now the great epitome of beauty. How he wished he could protect her so as to not let her be spoilt by the ravaging men who could easily take undue advantage and spoil her before she was fully mature mentally to hold her own and contain herself in this deceitful world. Also, as he was in the university, Ebuka understood how some lecturers intimidated female students into affairs by failing them in their courses. The cult mafias coerced babes into sacrileges and what not. The intricacies and despair of it all he understood and knew them all. After all, he had everything going for him, especially babes that flocked around him, considering his socio-economic background. Well, from what he had observed that afternoon, Ugomma seemed to be growing up quite fast and had assumed a lot of self-confidence, which meant sooner than later she would have to learn, know, and understand the world of men and still become the person she was destined to be.

Meanwhile, Ugomma lay on her back and gazed at the ceiling before drifting into sleep; in a frame of drowsy mind induced by the conquering power of sleep, she was thinking about the new guy with whom she had boarded the plane. 'He's not bad looking. Someday when school resumes, I will pay him a visit and find out the big deal about Eket beach and happenings around there that babes always gossip about in the hostel and the crazy interest that prompts them to go to Eket or PH. Some babes as a point of duty never spend weekends on campus, but hustle and jostle between these towns. Thank goodness, I've gotten my own contact now,' she meditated, then slept off.

Some hours later, about 7 p.m., a gentle tap at the door woke her up with a start. 'Ugomma, my daughter, that should be enough for now. I know you are really exhausted and need more rest, but let it be for the night so you don't wake up at midnight listening to the echoes of the night unable to sleep again till the morning.'

'Oh, Mama! Thanks for caring. I appreciate it. Please give me a couple of minutes and I will join you people downstairs.'

'That's all right, my dear. Your father just called on phone from overseas to know if you've returned safely to Lagos.'

In a couple of weeks, Ugomma acquired her personal character identification as a matured individual who now expressed herself in new styles in approach and mannerism, attending parties, picnics at the popular beach in Lagos, games at the national stadium on weekends, and other social functions, more so, in getting acquainted with and acquiring new friends.

Apparently, it was at one such picnic at Alpha Beach on the 12th of September that Ugomma met Richard, a U.S. resident holidaying in Nigeria, who like every one of them had an easy way with the local girls because of the crazy mental behaviour and apprehension they had about guys from abroad. Even if the guy was a grass mower, hewer of firewoods, or drawer of water in the USA and other European nations, those local babes did not want to know. Simply, dollar was the name of the game, and every one of them at the slightest opportunity would want to grab hers.

And conscious of this fragrant fact, boisterous about the exacerbated exchange rate of the dollar towering over the local naira currency, with a few dollars, those fun seekers and sugar-coated Nigerian- American home comers ravenously ravaged the psyche of the local ladies with vain promises of marriage and taking them to America. And having an edge of visiting their home of nativity with a return ticket, as soon as their money-bargaining power reduced in meeting up with the flashy false standard of flamboyancy and ostentation, they quietly sneaked out from the back door exit to the airport and flew back to God's own country.

Well, of course, to relocate from state to state or change telephone lines was as easy and convenient as the flipping of the hand. Therefore after enjoying such pleasant holidays, they return back to United States, whereas, their telephone lines become dead ends to where—gone and forgotten, forlorn loves. And in these days of husband scarcity in Nigeria, caused by the damaged economic environment, which had created a situation whereby graduates remained unemployed for years, the worst hit were the female ones, who got older at an alarming rate because of womanhood. One had to just mention marriage, and they would become an easy lay. Hence, men without moral uprightness could exploit them sexually. Thereby, you also saw the ladies contemporarily going to any lengths to treacherously and diabolically trap men into marriages that never lasted, because their foundations were not by God's will and because of pure human contracted love. Regrets and frustrations were their bane, so it was dubious and against the natural ordinance.

'Hi, babe! You look expensively pretty. May I have the honour of meeting you? My name is Richard, but my friends call me Richey. This is about the fifth day I'm holidaying in Nigeria from the United States of America, after three long years of absence?

'Is that right? Well, I'm Ugomma.' And without further introduction, Richey rambled and babbled along as if they'd been fellas from Adam.

'So what are you doing right now?' he asked, looking into her eyes and holding her hands in a firm grip.

'I'm a law student at the University of Uyo.'

'Where's that?' he queried.

'That's in Akwa Ibom State, after Aba city on the Calabar-Oron axis.' 'Okay, I understand. Invariably, I believe you've got no problems with academics.'

'No, not at least for now,' she responded.

'That's my darling. You see in America, the legal profession is such an attractive business because the average American is whole lot more aware about legalities and the rule of law and cannot be trampled upon by any fucking individual or government. Boy! Just go ahead and sue the bastard. So there are libel suits here and there. But the beauty of the American legal system is that justice is never delayed, unlike here in Nigeria where it's delayed and denied. You just wait and die, never getting a redress. May be they wish to appease the dead soul decades after as if the dead retain any sense of mortality.

That's fetishism which thrives in Africa and retards their mental development towards technological advancement as witnessed in other parts of the developed world.'

'Look, Richey, there's something about you.'

'What is it, baby?' he enquired.

'There's this exuberance of freedom hovering around you,' Ugomma observed.

'Yeah, darling, that's the American touch of liberty, which affects the soul and mental attitude of her citizens. The government over the years has altruistically created the enabling and ennobling environment for independence and actualisation of one's potentials to contributively build up the American dream of late Martin Luther King Jr.'

'Wonderful. I now see why all people across the world are wishing to coming to America,' opined Ugomma.

'Well, my baby Ugo, let's have a date. Why not check me up at Eko La Meriden hotel where I'm lodged in Suite 0419, Tuesday evening, say about 4 p.m.?'

'Richey, that will be nice seeing you again,' she said.

'Good evening, baby, catch you later.' He strolled away, humming a Kenny Rogers' tune—'I've found you'—walking to the farther part of the beach where he had parked his sports Benz car, under a cocoa-nut tree, while Ugomma rejoined her friends who were already getting set to go home, with the setting of the sun.

Throughout that weekend, Ugomma was in elated spirits, enmeshed in the excitement of meeting Richard Dike. The long vacation was turning out right for her. She was forever radiating and looking snazzy, cruising around in her mother's Honda car on most evenings, visiting her friends and attending parties without having any time for studies. In fact, her academics were in doldrums; she was in love with her beauty and savoured the glamour it accrued. She found it funny the way men stared at her, but without flinching, she regarded their overtures as a passing impulse.

Lying in bed on that Sunday night, reading a 'Mills and Boons' novel, her mind drifted to Richard, who had stirred up something in her as no man had ever affected her. She had read a lot about romances from the age of ten in those young days at Queens College. She has heard from the gossip of her room-mates in the university and about their escapades and exploits with men, in particular, those girls of Aba breed, who had polluted the University of Calabar and now UniUyo with their shabby dressing and behaviours. She had also watched blue films at one of her friends' home when their parents were away.

And now the woman in her was seriously yearning for liberation. The feel of a man's touch had recently raked her emotions. At eighteen years of age, Ugomma's body was fully grown up with all the contours and curves proportionately in perfect places. Unconsciously, she rose up from bed, moved in front of the dressing mirror, and pulled off her nightie, and as she was already not wearing a bra, she pulled down her white panties. Standing nude, she scrutinised her perfectly matured breasts with the tender nipples nudging erect stimulated by her gentle squeeze, the pubic hair stretching upwards a little above her navel, the long hands, and the fully round thighs. She gracefully turned round and in a flicker of a second loosened her hairs from the knotted ribbon, allowing them to settle on her broad shoulders. She looked at her pointed nose above her pomegranate red lips and smiled at herself, revealing deep dimples on both rosy cheeks that radiated perfect serenity on her face. Sauntering regally, she heaved a sigh and murmured gently, 'No woman, no matter how strikingly beautiful, is readily so except appreciated by a man. No wonder we feel so important and fulfilled when flattered by men's sweet nonsense talks. It actually creates a sense of belonging and confidence in us. Every woman likes to believe that she is needed and not wanted, used, and dumped like a toy,' she concluded. Slowly she wrapped herself up in a towel and walked into the bathroom; she showered to calm down her rebellious nerves and the straying thought of passions, then came back to the room, lay down, and slept off.

Monday, 13 September, was not much eventful. She accompanied her mother to Tejuosho market at Yaba for shopping. 'Mother!'

'Yes, darling,' her mum responded.

'Things seem quite expensive recently,' Ugomma observed.

'Apparently, my daughter, there's a terrible fluctuation and instability in the Nigerian price system, worsened by the unreliable transport system. Today there's fuel and tomorrow there will be artificial scarcity, created by greedy oil marketers, non-functional refineries, causing hike in transport fares with the multiple effects on the consumer goods and other essential services.'

'Mother, I think Nigerians are terrible opportunists. Everyone is in the quest of get-rich-quick syndrome and exploits situations to amass riches. The poverty level is just down at its ebb, and there's the stampede to run away from the poverty vice which has necessitated this contagious situation of "survival of the fittest". The poor masses in fact bear the entire brunt. And the strata of government does not seem to care.'

'My dear, the worst culprit is the local government council, which is supposed to bring the goodies of governance to the grassroots. May be someone needs to educate them of their actual responsibilities. Ugomma, why don't you acquire some sets of new undies?'

'Yes, Mum, there are some designer wears I noticed in that shop.'

'Okay, let's get them for you.' After buying the panties and other personal effects for Ugomma, they completed their shopping and drove back home through Adekunle Road to Third Mainland Bridge, Obalende Falomo Bridge to Victoria Island.

That evening, Ugomma and her brother played hide and seek game in the swimming pool for almost two hours, after which they also played the chess game. Dinner was another celebration of a family get-together, because their cousin, Ogechi, and his parents visited from Surulere. Just before sleeping, Ugomma was fanaticising about her date with Richard the next day. It was an appointment she had resolved to keep, no matter what. On the morrow therefore, after the family breakfast, she went to the saloon to fix her hair into a special style and manicured her nails. By the time she returned home at 1.15 p.m., Ebuka, who was watching a film in the living room with his girlfriend, Rebecca, Maraako, and Uchendu, was stunned. Spontaneously, he sprang to his feet, stretching out his hands towards Ugomma for a hug, and announced, 'Here comes our Lady Diana!'

Ugomma hilariously embraced her brother, while Maraako and Uchendu whistled in approval of their princess. 'Rebecca, how are you doing? It's nice to have you around. How have you been enjoying the holidays?'

Rebecca could not help feeling jealous of Ugomma, because she was not only the only daughter of that rich family, but also at the way her brothers adoringly loved her; she warmly responded, 'I'm fine, and thanks for caring.'

Ugomma left to go to her room upstairs to catch a nap before her 4 p.m. date. She woke up at 3.30 p.m., took a proper bath, and carefully selected one of the latest designer undies she had bought yesterday—a pink-coloured bra and panties which had rose flowers embroidered on them. She wore a beautiful brown evening gown, with a fine leather black bag and shoes to match. She carried 5,000 naira in 200 naira denomination in her purse. The fragrance of her designer perfume was pleasant but enduring.

When she came downstairs at about 3.45 p.m., she saw Uchendu sleeping on the sofa, and she called out to Felicia, their house help, 'Where are my brothers?'

'Ebuka drove out with Rebecca while Maraako has gone out to play soccer,' she replied.

'Well, when Mama comes back, inform her that I've gone visiting with my friend Yetunde at Queen's Drive, Ikoyi, and that I will be back later in the evening.'

'Okay, Ugomma.'

'Meanwhile, buy yourself something with this 200 naira.'

'Ah, Ugo thanks for being generous as usual.'

'You are welcome, Felicia, and take care of the house O!' She decided against driving her mother's other car, but walked off to their Uboma Close exit gate, flagged down a taxi, and headed for Eko La Meriden hotel.

At 3.55 p.m., the taxi pulled up at the hotel's car park. Ugomma paid off the driver and briskly walked into the lobby. She became the censure of all eyes around, especially the men who abruptly stopped in their tracks, staring at her. The ladies also couldn't help looking at her; conscious of her surroundings and the way the female receptionists had started gossiping about her because of the men lusting after her, she blushed and wished the lift would just descend and rescue her before the men with their penetrating eyes stripped her nude. At that instance, with a buzzing sound the lift jacked open and she rushed into a corner of the lift, allowing room for other occupants. She asked the operator to drop her off at the fourth floor. Consequently at exactly 4 p.m., Ugomma was standing in front of the door marked room 0419. She gently tapped on the door twice, and there stood Richey, holding ajar the door, smiling mischievously. 'Come on in, my sweet angel he greeted her.

'Thanks, Richey. How was your day?'

'Fine, darling? He shut the door and leant back, watching Ugomma with intense concentration as if conjuring her picture in his mind. Immediately, Ugomma felt alone and turned sharply only to observe Richey in that position staring at her.

Her heart skipped and she queried him, 'Richey, what's the problem?' 'No, baby, there's no problem. I never found you this breathtakingly beautiful the other day at the beach, probably because of the swimming trunks you wore.' He reached her and passionately planted a full-mouthed kiss on her lips, which calmed her down and evaporated her doubts.

'You know, Ugomma, since last Saturday when we met at the Alpha Beach, you have filled my moments and thoughts. I just couldn't wait for this day that has become real now, so please feel at home.'

'Thanks, Richey, for caring. I also have been thinking about you.'

'Sure, baby, that makes the two of us. Let's get us something to eat and drink. You know, I've ordered my lunch to be brought up here, including drinks.'

'Oh, that's fine,' she responded, 'but I can only eat a little food and share the red wine.'

'There's no problem. Your wish is my command.' After the food, while they were toasting the wine, listening to a blues rhythm from the music set, which softly soothed the moment, and with the air conditioner oozing its buzzing sounds, Ugomma's heart began to pound. Richey sensing her changed mood asked her what seemed like a funny question, 'Ugomma, are you a good cook?'

'O Richey, come of it! What kind of question is that for a big girl like me?'

'Look, baby, I didn't mean to insult you, but please do answer me precisely.'

'Yes, of course, even with the house-help in the house, my mother ensured that she taught and groomed me up well domestically.'

'Fine, my dear. There's something irrelevant, but it means a lot to me in the cooking process that I would love you to do now.' Ugomma could not understand Richey's thought flow, therefore had an innocent blank expression. Richey laughed mischievously at her, drawing her closer, and kissed her again.

'Richey, you are enjoying yourself playing games with me, isn't it?'

'Baby, I want you to feel relaxed. Some moments ago, you looked so tensed up.' But in her mind, Ugomma was wondering how and when Richey would charge up on her; according to her, he was delaying the action. But Richey, being well experienced with women like an actor, was playing out some scenes sequentially. Suddenly, he stood up deliberately from the bed, dragging Ugomma with him, stepped outside, and asked Ugomma to practice the exercise of peeling off the onions. The moment she had fantasised before now stared right there in her face. She couldn't muster the courage to pull off her clothes before a guy. Reality was more than her braggadocio.

'Richey, why don't you help me out?' she pleaded. Taking her dress off, he left only her bra and panties on. She shyly traced Richey's gaze to her abdomen where a few hairs lay smooth. He ordered her to turn around and gently unhooked her bra which gave way obediently. Now only the cover of her treasure island was left, and she closed her eyes as Richey's masterly hands moved around her hips and pulled down the pink rose-designed panties, and she cooperated, lifting her legs to allow it to drop on the carpet, still with her eyes shut.

Richey withdrew back a step and savoured her beautiful curved body with his shining eyes and exclaimed, '*Wa-wa* O! Baby, I have not seen a beauty like you yet all my life.' Touching the threshold of her cunt, he pulled her pubic hair fondly, and Ugomma opened her eyes, smiling innocently. This response spurred an animated frenzy in Richey as he rushed into sporadic sensual actions. He picked up Ugomma and gently laid her on the bed, kneeling down over her, and started working on her with his hands and tongue. Thrusting his hands into the hollow of her armpits, he caressed her erect nipples with his tongue, slowly but steadily descending kisses down her navel. Ugomma was now shaking with a pleasure that she never knew was embedded in her sensuality. Bringing his hand into her pussy, she expectantly opened her long legs, inviting him in. But Richey was not in a hurry to take her yet; rather, his tongue slipped into the threshold of her cunt, sending jitters all over her body system. As he massaged her erect clitoris, that was the most flaming sensuality she had ever experienced. Jacking nervously, she sensed an explosion inside her brain, which quivered her entire body system, knocking her drained and satisfying the crescendo of orgasm. The soft moaning momentarily stopped as she tenderly cuddled Richey's hairy chest with her right hand. She had read many 'Mills and Boons' romance literatures, watched films, but they were nothing like what Richey was doing to her now.

'Ugomma!'

'Yes, Richey,' she answered.

'You mean you are still a virgin?'

'You have discovered that, is it not?' she asked him.

'Baby, I'm thrilled.' As he kissed her now more intimately, it kindled a steaming desire in Ugomma as she pulled him down on her. Richey could hold back no more; he took her and became the first man to have a sexual relationship with her. She never knew the baptism of sexual pleasure mingled with pain and joy. The reality of it all made her feel hollow.

'Richey, it's about 7 p.m. and I should be going back home.'

'Okay, Ugo baby, I am sure going to take you home.'

'No, please, I wouldn't want my parents to start interrogating me about you. More so, I left a message that I was visiting my girlfriend at Ikoyi when I left home. So don't bother accompanying me home. Thanks for caring all the same.'

'Okay, Ugomma, your wish is my command.' As she was dressed up and now about to leave, Richey handed 500 dollars to Ugomma.

'Ah! Richey, you should not bother yourself with all these. I have enough to spare. Money is not my problem. My family is quite comfortable.' He was pleasantly surprised that a girl in contemporary Nigeria was refusing the offer of American dollars whereas others would have jumped and grabbed the offer. This actually impressed him to beg her to accept the gesture.

'Ugomma, I respect your feelings and doff my hat for you, but please accept this token from me.'

'Well, thank you all the same.' She collected the money and tucked it inside her bag. He also gave her an expensive Omega wristwatch. Together they stepped out into the corridor and Richey locked his suite, then they strolled to the elevator. He pressed the button and it jacked open for them to enter, and they descended down to the busy lobby. Richey pleasantly held her hand and walked her outside to the hotel gate. He stopped a taxi and held the door for Ugomma to enter in. That done, he bent low and kissed her good night with the promise of keeping in touch with her. And the cab sped off.

As she rode home, Ugomma opened her bag and brought out the complimentary card Richey had given her; while studying it, a thought came to her mind and she began to wonder how much she knew about him, the stranger she had sold her prized virginity to irretrievably forever. At the entrance of their close, she paid off the taxi driver and walked down home. She entered their compound by 7.30 p.m. The floodlights mounted at the far end of the fence illuminated the entire surroundings; crossing the grass lawn, she entered the house.

'Good evening, Mama she greeted her mother, who gave a searching look at her as if searching her soul at that instance.

'Hello! Ugomma, where have you been all this evening?' she queried. 'I went visiting Yetunde, my friend, at Queen's Drive, Ikoyi,' she lied.

'Even at that, you overstayed, Ugomma. I expected you home before now,' her mother insisted because she noticed something strange about her daughter's shining eyes and mannerism this evening. And as she did not want to drag the matter further in the presence of her sons, she decided to let her go for the moment.

'Welcome back, Sister Ugo,' her kid brothers greeted her.

'Hi, guys, how are you doing?' She mounted the staircase and walked into her room; she shut her bedroom door, flung her bag on the bed, kicked off her shoes, removed her wristwatch, undressed, and walked into the bathroom. She ran hot water from the heater and mixed it with cold water to the temperature suited to her aching body, then she dipped herself into the bathtub to soothe her body, especially her tender breasts that Richey had teased. She gently massaged her nipples and abdomen regions and scrubbed herself thoroughly, and satisfied that she was decently freshened up, she stepped out and cleaned herself up. She also took two tablets of aspirin and walked back to her room. After rubbing cream and deodorant, she dressed in her nightie, lay on her bed, and slept off without bothering about dinner. At about 8.45 p.m., Ebuka drove into the compound, from his own outing.

Precisely about 4.15 a.m. at the dawn of the next day, Wednesday 15 September, Mrs Uboma woke up her daughter with a gentle tap on her shoulder. Drowsily, she sat up on the bed resting her back against the wall, facing her mother. 'Ugomma!'

'Yes, Mum she answered.

'Can you now tell me the whole truth of your whereabouts yesterday afternoon?' she queried.

'I am sorry, Mum. I lied to you yesterday night.'

'I know. Sure, you could not fool me. As your mother I am old enough to observe and know sex written all over you the moment you entered the sitting room. The stench of it trailed you, regardless of the fragrance of your perfume.' Ugomma broke down; crying convulsively, she confessed to her mother about the entire episode with Richard, how they had met and everything that had transpired between them. 'Listen, Ugomma, now you have lost your virginity to a guy, rather to a stranger, because of stupid curiosity and exciting adventure. Your inestimable treasure of pride is now forever lost to a stranger on a platter of gold, someone you know little or nothing about his background or personality, a person who might take you for granted and forgotten as another victim of passing impulse. It's quite unfortunate. You better not start indulging in premarital sex, because it is almost difficult to hold back after the first experience. It becomes a snare as a reoccurring decimal.' Advising her to be cautious against becoming pregnant and bringing shame to the family, she said, 'Ugomma, you must not drag the good name of this family into the mud. You are sent to the university to become a better qualified human being and bring honour to the family, and not flirt about with men. In our days, we upheld high moral standards and pursued our educational priority with vigour and fear of God. And that is why my husband respects, trusts, and cherishes me the more, because he was my first lover. But you children of the jet generation are in daring rush for everything and can easily sell off your conscience in the name of bragging. That brevity I regard as foolishness. When you have enjoyed all the pleasure and ostentations in a crazy rush of thirty-five years, what is there any more to live for? And that is why they behave as if they don't wish to live up to the old age which their demeanours depict as a burden.'

While she was still sobbing, her mother reminded her of that young man who had come to the local airport with her on that day from school and how she had been flirting with him. 'More so, who is the Tony that called you yesterday from Onitsha while you were out?'

'He is my boyfriend in the university,' Ugomma responded. She invariably told her mother all about Tony and her other friends at school. She apologised and pleaded with her mother not to tell her father of it when he returned from his trip.

'That's all right, Ugomma, because there is no confidence for anyone who do not feel remorse over wrongdoings. So set your mind in coming with me to the hospital for medical attention later in the morning at 9 a.m.'

'Okay, Mum. Thanks for caring.' Her mother left her and closed the door behind her.

In the next couple of weeks, Ugomma became of sober demeanour; the innuendo juxtaposed her psycho logical disposition, which disenchanted her usual boisterous approaches. This her mother observed and felt happy within that Ugomma had learnt from the past incident. As there was no need for wallowing in self-pity and crying over spilt milk, that evening of 28 September after dinner, Mrs Uboma took her daughter aside alone to relax in the garden beside their swimming pool under the radiance of the moonlight, while her sons watched a home video of *Ashes of Hatred* written and produced by Emmanuel K. Ayalaogu, one of the renowned script writers in the film industry of Nigeria. Moreover, she didn't want the foregoing to strain the beautiful cordial relationship between them, so she tried to give her a pep talk and nip that tendency in the bud. 'Ugomma, in the past few weeks, I have observed you have not been as happy and graceful as usual. You have also lost some weight, which is not good for you while on vacation.'

'Mother, thank you. I am fine. Concerning losing weight, I think it's because I spend more time in swimming lately.'

'Look, Ugomma, I am your mother and shall be failing in my duty if I should close my eyes or not bother about your health and welfare, especially now that you are on holidays. And I wouldn't want your father to return back to Nigeria and meet you in this sickly state. Hence, I would advise you stop brooding over the past incident. As a matter of fact, Ugomma, you can easily go astray, but it's hard to reconstruct, so stop crying, but be careful of what you do with your womanhood, henceforth. And be more prayerful for *no one stumbles on bended knees,* okay?'

'Thanks, Mum, I will remember that.'

That same night around 11 p.m., Igwe phoned from overseas, informing his family that he would be back the next two days, having completed his business transaction. He would be aboard the KLM flight scheduled to arrive at Muritala Mohammed International Airport at 7.15 p.m. on Friday, 30 September.

Lolo Uboma in the next few days busied herself and the entire household with the gay preparation for Igwe's return home. That night, Igwe returned home to the warm embrace of his family after a six-week's business trip of Europe, Asia, and America. It was celebration time with pomp and pageantry in galore. The entire household was galvanised into joy, especially Lolo who had successfully managed her husband's business empire and the home front all this long.

Their telephone lines became hotlines as friends and relations bombarded them with congratulatory messages besides those that physically visited them. Later that night when all guests had gone away, Igwe called his family together in the sitting room. 'Lolo, I want to thank you all for everything, but especially for having held fort this long I was away.'

'Oh, darling, you are most welcome.'

'Ugomma, how was your exam?' he enquired.

'Dad, there wasn't any problem.'

'Ebuka, Maraako, and Uchendu, how have you guys been faring too?'

'Well, Dad, I have moved into my final year now, so when school resumes I will be more occupied. I have already started writing my project work.'

'Oh, that's good,' Igwe responded. 'Maraako, your mother told me that you have successfully gained admission also into the University of Nigeria, Nsukka, to study medicine and surgery, which means you will be joining Ebuka there.'

'Yes, Dad,' he responded.

'Uchendu, you should be sitting for your senior secondary school certificate exams next May June.'

'Yes, Daddy,' he replied.

'Well, to God be the glory and kudos to all of you. I am proud of you all, okay?' He also informed them of how successful his trip was, then gave them their respective gifts and had a brief family devotion. Then he took leave of them and walked upstairs to his master bedroom. After dispatching the children, Lolo joined her husband in their room.

'Lolo, you are a wife out of a million, a diadem in the galaxies of stars. You have done marvellously well this long while. In fact, I believe in you. You know at times I think of what my life would have been without such an understanding wife like you?

'Eh-woo "Ezigbo dim", thanks for appreciating me. I am encouraged so wonderfully. Without any doubt, I believed you from day one, way back in the university when you proposed after our early friendship. Although you had a humble beginning, something in me assured me that you are meant for greatness. And every opportunity, you exhibited a glimpse of confidence and mental approach focused on actualising those goals no matter the odds. That's what I cherish most and I am not disappointed. Thanks, my beloved wife, after due consideration, I convinced myself that life is just all about adjustment, comportment, and supreme services, for man is at best in close relationship with God and service to God and humanity.'

In the next couple of weeks ahead, Igwe glowed in absolute good health and dexterity, radiating great confidence and joviality. And he focused on the arrangements of building a factory site on the outskirts of Lagos-Ejigbo. He packaged, negotiated, and convinced his foreign partners to come and avail themselves of the business opportunity existing in contemporary Nigeria as the greatest market in Africa. In particular, the democratic dispensation had created an enabling political environment for genuine businesses to flourish, considering the abundant human and natural resources there. In the past, the crux of the matter was whom to trust. No doubt, therefore, that Igwe Uboma was one of the most credible Nigerians living; his broadbased nationality and structural functionality were identified as track records which made his name a password both at home and abroad. No wonder the greatness and affluence of the Ubomas were soaring high in all spheres of life now.

Chapter Five

Ugomma returned to school for her second year in the university. Taking stock of the vacation that had been filled with various activities that had changed her outlook to life in all ramifications, she came to a personal conviction and conclusion that things would never be the same again. In the second year, she was allocated a new hall of residence and room with different room-mates, especially babes from Aba and Port Harcourt, namely, Ezinne Chetta, Ogechi Atum, two final-year students—Mercy Nwosu from Ihitte-Uboma L.G.A, Imo State, and Uduak Nwa from Ona L.G.A; Akwa Ibom State—both in the accounting department, and her former room-mates Yetunde and Fatima. Her beloved friend Mfon was separated from her and was now in Hall W4 Room 6.

Tony and Emeka, now as final-year students, sold off their bed spaces in the hostel HM IA Room 19, and rented an apartment in town. During the first two weeks of resumption, students returned enmass, as both campuses bubbled with everyone rushing to check results and registration of new courses. The new Jambites (freshmen) were not left out as this was the beginning of a new academic session.

'Hi, Mfon, how was the holiday? I hope you had a swell time,' Ugomma asked.

'Yes, dear, it was a wonderful exciting period for me all through.'

'Sorry, you didn't get me all the time you called.'

'Not to worry, my mother passed your messages to me. Congratulations, your father has established another industry—a manufacturing outfit. He was on line with my father two weeks ago.'

'Mfon dear, my father now is busy than ever before with his foreign partners around in the country. It's one engagement or the other that involves touring to Port Harcourt today or Abuja the next day. In fact, his business empire is expanding with more connections. Even my mother is not spared this time around. Thank goodness, they are no more bearing children. So, beloved, how are your folks?'

'They are okay,' responded Mfon.

Changing the topic of discussion at this juncture, Mfon informed Ugomma that Emeka had formally visited her parents during the holidays and that they were happily disposed to him and his parents. Ugomma was shocked and expressed the same to Mfon. 'Mfon, it's a lie. You can't be kidding me!'

'Ugo, it's true. You know I wouldn't lie to you. Look at the engagement ring he gave to me.' Ugomma was overwhelmed and embraced Mfon, rocking her backwards and forwards momentarily before disengaging from each other. As tears of joy rolled down the cheeks of Mfon, Ugomma pulled out her white handkerchief and wiped them off. 'Ugomma, I know you love reading poems. Just go through this beautiful piece that Emeka wrote for me:

Love is the ocean
Love is the Victoria Falls
Which velocity dams the height?
That radiates the mind
But which reason guides
Ascending to the realms of understanding
The rushing passions of youths under flows
Into the tributaries of live experiences
As unto wide ocean of love
Maturity ploys and explores
Like the green bar-tree
That produces its fruits in all seasons
The leaves never wither
'Cause it is nourished from the fertility
Of enlightened mind that cares
Come on then, sweetheart
Let's swim in this ocean
That courage and trust—
Navigators, washes us ashore
Where the natural sea breeze
Cuddle our souls to ever fulfilment.'

After reading through, Ugomma exclaimed, 'What a consonance rhapsody of love! Mfon, you mean that Emeka wrote this wonderful piece for you?'

'Yes, my dear,' responded Mfon.

'I'm not surprised because you can see it in his eyes that he dearly loves you and can't afford losing you to any other man, no matter what.'

'You're right, Ugomma, no need chasing after wild goose. These days men are not forthright about marriage because of poor economic reality in the country. And the worst off are the spinsters who are easily and fast growing older, as young girls grow rapidly and more beautiful. In fact, I can't bear losing Emeka to another woman, so I've urged him for us to formally be engaged before he graduates?

'You mean you actually encouraged him for these steps taken so far?' Ugomma asked.

'Yes o! Mfon answered satisfied, giving a smile of fulfilment.

'That's great! I wish both of you a wonderful happy marriage life soon?

'Thanks, Ugomma,' she responded. 'Sweetheart, tell me your experience this past vac. How did it fare with you?' Without much ado, Ugomma narrated to her about Stephen Daniels, whom she had met on the day she was returning to Lagos for the long vacation and who worked at Mobil QIT Eket, and that she hoped tracing him soon after settling down in this new semester. She also told Mfon about Richmond, the Nigerian-American who deflowered her at Eko la Meridian Hotel, last September.

'He promised me great things in future, even proposing marriage at that instance? But instead of applauding her, Mfon was shocked and displeased at the turn of events in Ugomma's life just within the past two months and more.

'Look, Ugomma, you've made a terrible mistake by falling victim to these never serious-Nigerian-Americans who come on vacation in

Nigeria. They go about deceiving gluttonous materialistic girls into make-believe marriage that can never be. As soon as they satisfy their sexual escapades, they throw money around and vamoose into thin air and oblivion. Worse still, a lot of them are married to American ladies who wouldn't tolerate them marrying a second wife, else they would blow up their heads as cheats. So these countrymen are conscious of that fact and play safe, taking advantage of local girls whose lusts make them vulnerable to such ramblers.'

'Mfon, you may be right because there is something about this guy. He seems to be smart and down-to-earth and caring.'

'Look, Ugomma, those are facades of the fox. Underneath, they are raving wolves. Believe me, just last year, one of our female students called Idara in the English department fell victim to this vice. This particular guy paraded her all over the place. They actually did the traditional marriage that was well attended by all and sundry, especially the cream of Akwa Ibom society. But after the fanfare, the big boy Alingo flew back to the United States and till date has never bothered communicating with this babe. Hence, all over Eastern Nigeria in particular, wise ladies and those made wise because of such incidents have come to accept the fact that a bird in hand is better than a thousand in the bush.'

'My sister, let's fashy that angle,' said Ugomma. 'When did you see Emeka last?' she enquired from Mfon.

'Yesterday. Yea, that reminds me Emeka and Tony resolved to rent an apartment off campus along Barracks Road. There is this new private hostel facility with modern equipment called the Eureka Peace Lodge, built by a business mogul residing in Lagos. Remarkably, in response to the Federal Government clarion call for such ventures to ameliorate the accommodation problems in the universities, good- spirited Nigerians are becoming responsive and making fast returns on such laudable ventures.'

'So that's where Tony and Emeka are residing as big boys. Mfon, do you know that Tony called my home during the holidays and it was my mother that received the call? And of course, trust her, she asked me all about him.'

'Really!' asked Mfon. 'What then did you tell her about Tony?'

'Well, of course, all there is about Tony and his proposal.'

'And what did your mother advise?'

'She advised me to be careful and not rush into something I will regret later. But to maintain good relationship with nice friends, and factually, the choice and decision to make is mine, who knows better the people I associate with.'

'Look, Ugo, take note of this, all men are made, but wait for their own manifestation of glory. That is to say, that to everyone there is his or her time in life. Some people's morning is dawn in the early stage of their existence, while to others the noon middle stage, and to another the evening setting sun of their old age. They enjoy and die happily. All depends on destiny, vision, and inspirational approach of each individual. Even then, the Holy Scriptures in the Book of Ecclesiastes 9:11 reads, "The race is not for the swift, nor the battle for the strong, neither bread to the wise, nor riches to the men of understanding nor yet favour to men of skill, but time and chance happens to them all." In fact, all is of God.'

'Thanks, Mfon, we've had enough for now. Let's go have lunch.'
'That's okay with me. Let's go.'

After the meal, they returned back to Mfon's room 6 Hall W4 at about 3.45 p.m. 'Ugomma, remember that we are visiting Emeka and Tony later this evening.'

'That's true. What time should be appropriate?' Ugomma asked.

Then Mfon responded, '6 p.m. should be all right by me.'

'That suits me too. Why don't you meet me up then?' Ugomma asked.

'Fine, I'll be with you by 4.45 p.m.' Mfon saw her friend off to her hall's common room and went back to her room, while Ugomma returned to her room at W5 Room 20.

'Hi, Ugomma, where have you been?' her new room-mate Ogechi asked.

'Oge, I'd just gone to have my lunch,' responded Ugomma, who then lay down on her bed and pulled out a *Heart* magazine to relax with before falling asleep.

At this period in time, academic work had not commenced, thereby affording students lots of leisure and time to socialise. Ugomma was still sleeping when Mfon came to wake her up at 5.30 p.m. for the scheduled visit. 'Ugo dear,' Mfon called her with a gentle shake to her shoulder.

And she woke up with a start, asking her, 'What's the time?' Mfon informed her that they had thirty minutes before departure time. So Ugomma rushed to take her bath while Mfon engaged herself with the same magazine as she listened to the soft tune of classical music from Ugomma's compact disc.

That done, Ugomma returned to the room in the next fifteen minutes and got dressed, and off they went, after she had introduced Mfon to her room-mates who were available. 'Mercy, Uduak, Ogechi, Ezinne, and Chinyere, please meet my beloved friend and sister, Mfon?

'Hi, Mfon,' they chorused.

'It's my pleasure meeting you all,' Mfon replied.

'In fact, she's my Nwanne-di-na-mba. Right from my day one in this university, she has always been there for me. And our fathers were actually course mates in Unilag, and ever since, we have been family friends,' Ugomma explained.

'That's great, and that is what good friendship should be,' opined Mercy.

'You know what, today I and Mfon are best of friends and course mates in law,' continued Ugomma.

'Wonderful, and I guess your children also will continue the tradition.' They all laughed at Uduak's sense of humour, as Ugomma and Mfon stepped outside, closing the door behind them.

Walking out from the common room to outside, Mfon observed how the flowers in the compound had blossomed; their buds were flourishing like the Beulah Land. In particular, the pride of Barbados standing in front of the accounting departmental block looked like a bride on her honeymoon, while the queen of the night stood adjacently in front of Hall W5, oozing out her scent which the gentle breeze spread around. Even the whispering tree hummed in the noon of Harmattan season. The scenario all over the two campuses at this time and season of the year when the rainy season was gradually subsiding was a blend of various colours. What a heaven for the horticulturists!

'Mfon, do you know that whenever I perceive this scent, it tickles my sense of womanhood?'

'Why? You sound strange, Ugomma. Really! It's just like the smell of mowed grasses in the morning during August break.'

'Look, Mfon, I experienced the reality of life through things that would not matter or make sense to the ordinary person.'

Approaching the annex exit gate, they flagged down two okada riders and mounted the motorbikes which zoomed off to Barracks Road. They disembarked and paid off the riders and climbed the staircase to the second floor.

'Look, Mfon, I like this environment. It looks decent and not congested like the hostels. I think it will be nice to negotiate with Tony and Emeka to transfer this place to us when they eventually graduate.' 'Ugomma, it's a nice idea.'

'Remember to discuss it with them so that they introduce us to their landlord when the time comes.'

'Yes, Ugomma, here we are. The next room down the corridor on the extreme right is their room. And it looks like they are home.'

'That is okay,' Ugomma responded. Mfon tapped gently on the door, and Emeka's voice invited them in.

'So nice seeing you again,' she responded heartily.

'What about Tony?' Ugomma asked.

'He's visiting a neighbour on the third floor. Excuse me while I inform him that you babes are here.'

Emeka left the apartment to call Tony. 'Look, Tony, I've got a pleasant surprise for you. Guess who are in the room right now?' Emeka teased Tony.

'Eh-Em! That should be Mfon and Ugomma.'

'Boy!' Emeka exclaimed. 'You are perfectly right.' Without wasting more time, they both rushed down into their apartment.

'Mine, O mine, Ugomma darling, what a pleasure seeing you again!' Tony greeted her with hands wide open. Ugomma instantaneously stepped into his warm embrace, smiling. 'Baby! You look well fed and taken care of. Your mother must have stuff you with lots of goodies all through the vac.'

'Yes, Tony, I had a swell time,' Ugomma responded. Mfon and Emeka were smiling approvingly at the warm disposition displayed by Tony and Ugomma.

'This happy reunion calls for celebrations,' said Tony, as he opened the fridge and brought out Eva red wine. He opened it and poured out the drink into four glasses on the table beside Emeka. And they toasted cheers to their solidarity and safe return to a new academic year.

'Cheers!' they all responded. Later, Mfon and Ugomma entered the kitchen and prepared dinner; they all ate with gaiety and gist till about 8 p.m. when Ugomma and Mfon went back to the campus.

In the following couple of weeks, all the results of the past semester were published in different departments. Emeka and Tony had no problem, since they had built their GPA up to a 3.74 and 3.98, respectively. Mfon's and Ugomma's results were very encouraging. Hence, cumulatively Mfon had 3.78 while Ugomma had 4.20 in year 1. And now in year 2, they both aspired to work harder either to maintain their performance or possibly advance to higher standards. Because the higher they were, the tougher and wider the scope of learning.

By mid-November, lectures had resumed in earnest; lecturers had commenced giving assignments in various courses, thereby necessitating students to use the libraries more often for research, except the NFAS (No Future Ambition Students) who allowed their course works and assignments to pile up due to their truancy and incessant travel to big cities or unnecessary gallivanting from campus to campus busy doing nothing.

Maybe those cult guys, carrying out their clandestine activities from one university campus to another, did waste time around. On Thursday, 5 p.m., Ugomma was in her room updating her notes on contract law when she overheard her room-mates, Ogechi and Onome, gist about their visit to Eket two days ago. 'Onome, have you gone to check your results?' Ogechi asked.

'Yes,' she responded. 'Do you know that I visited Uyo during the holidays to see Mr Bragado of Business Management? I brought him some gifts, and he had sex with me and still failed me in that course.'

'But that is not fair,' responded Ogechi. 'You see some of these lecturers, you need to be careful when dealing with them. Some after paying their charges give you C grade instead of A or B. At times, they behave as if they have not had any relationship with you at all or shared any intimacy with you.'

'Well, I will try to work hard this time around and pass that course. Even if I make a D or E, let my people go, I don't mind. But enough with that fox lecturer,' responded Onome.

'Despite that, my friend, sorting is the name of the game for the NFAs. You read to know, but sort to pass your exams, period,' said Ogechi. 'It was in year 2, I learnt that lesson and resolved never to fall "mogu" to any lecturer again, because by the time you start having carry-overs, how many lecturers do you want to sleep with? Maybe yes for the men, but what do you do with the female lecturers?' Ogechi asked.

'You have a point there, Oge,' replied Onome. 'The female lecturers are nightmares when it comes to things like that. They prefer dealing with guys, but will not compromise anything for us. In fact, I wonder how women could hate their gender. You observe them being so harsh as if you are about to snatch their husbands or boyfriends away from them.'

Their despair drifted away as they changed the course of discussion to Onome's visit to Eket on Tuesday. This also Ugomma paid attention to as she listened along. 'Thank goodness I met with Larry before break time.'

'That means both of you went to lunch together?' Ogechi asked.

'Yes, of course, I got to Eket around 10.45 a.m. and by 11 a.m. on the dot entered his office. Although he was not expecting me, all the same I was welcomed. He knows that students are also cash-trapped and constrained during this period of the semester. Even some are now operating on 1-0-1 meal? Onome showed her friend the 5,000 naira and narrated the fun escapade after lunch when Larry took her to a guest house in town.

'Baby! Congratulations. You sure had a nice time. For me, I'm going to travel to Port Harcourt tomorrow after my 12 noon lecture,' said Ogechi.

'That means that you will bust the lecture for 2 p.m.?' Onome asked.

'*Nne!* Forget that, I will borrow notes from Judith my course mate when I return next week Monday.'

'That's all right!' Onome responded. While the duo were discussing, Ugomma had a flashback. She remembered Stephen Daniel, that ebony guy that worked with Mobil QIT and whom she had met while going back to Lagos last semester. She suspended what she was doing and searched earnestly for his complimentary card; she found it in her handbag. She studied it and decided visiting him the following week.

That evening, she visited Tony and found him alone in the apartment. 'Who's in here?' she greeted, knocking at the door.

'Come on in if you're beautiful and rich,' Tony jokingly responded.

'Good evening, Tony dear.'

'Wonderful, Ugomma, my beautiful angel. You're highly welcome.' He kissed her passionately. 'I was just thinking of you some moments ago.'

'Well, here we are,' she responded.

'Do make yourself comfortable. There are some drinks in the fridge— wine, orange juice, and digestive biscuits. Serve yourself.'

'That's great, Tony You guys are really enjoying yourselves out here. There's obviously a great difference living off campus. You enjoy lots of privacy, comfort and cook your meals, unlike the crowded hostels, with regular don'ts. Even babes could be really messy.'

'Yes, of course, here you're in your own world. Even at that, you babes still cook in the hostels with electric boiling rings,' replied Tony.

'You're right, my dear,' said Ugomma. 'Nevertheless, Tony, I would love to take over here when you and Emeka have graduated. In fact, I discussed that with Mfon the last time we visited.'

'That's good idea,' Tony agreed. 'Are you going to live with Mfon, your friend?' he enquired.

'No, I would prefer staying alone. Moreover, Mfon's parents will not allow their daughter to live off campus.'

'Still all right! That means I can and will visit you here after graduation.'

'Sure!' Ugomma replied.

While they were discussing, Tony had started caressing her. She did not rebuff him. 'Tony, before you go further, why don't you shut that door?' He obliged. Ugomma's reserved and aloof attitude towards Tony's sexual advances in the previous semester gave way to her now receptive and yielding responses which overwhelmed him, matching him in every rhapsodic animated sensual overtures. In the very end, they reached a crescendo that flushed them into satisfaction. Tony could hardly believe his luck. 'Am I dreaming?' he queried his mind. And to be sure that this was real, they had another round of intercourse; this time, it was lovemaking and not sex. They both relaxed, giving all, and had full pleasure that they would ever remember. Tony savoured and explored all treasures she'd got and found her a match in all dimensions. Tony had discovered the real Ugomma, enjoyed her scintillating tender body, but he would be satisfied owning her for life. But Ugomma would not allow that thought to dwell in her mind even for a while, because she thought herself to be young and did not want to be hooked down to any man's wishes and caprices. She still wanted to explore the world and master her passions and emotional ends and be able to express herself whenever the need arose.

'Ugomma, you know that I love you?' Tony asked.

'You asked me the same question some time ago.'

'I will love it that you marry me then said Tony.

Ugomma gently lifted herself up from Tony's chest, and looking into his eyes, she said, 'Tony, I've come to love you. I respect your perseverance and genuine care. But please give this matter a hiatus. Talk this marriage stuff out of our relationship. Honestly, I don't envisage marriage in the next five years or more.'

'Look! Ugo darling, it's as if you are talking soul. I don't think there's anything wrong with making up with both of us now. Reasonably, your friend Mfon and Emeka have got formally engaged. That doesn't in any way impede their studies. Rather, they have stocked hope and faithfulness for a greater tomorrow. More so, coming from the same university orientation, they would have lots of great stories to flow together. But please, don't be fooled by the fantasy of exploring the world, because by the time you're through, a lot would have also gone through you and leave prints of frivolities, with despair and regrets remaining indelible on your mind.'

'Well spoken, Tony, but please hold your peace. It has not come to that situation yet.'

'You sounded offended, darling. I don't mean to hurt or castigate you, but remember I told you.'

Ugomma took a cold shower and decided to go back to the campus around 8.45 p.m. Tony had resolved not to bother her any more with the marriage issue; after all, what would be would be. Together they strolled down the staircase to the main road. Tony stopped a motorcyclist and paid him; he gave Ugomma a peck on her cheek as she climbed unto it. 'Look, Okada, drive with care O!' he instructed the man. 'Ugomma, thanks for coming and have a pleasant evening.'

'You too, Tony!' The motorcyclist sped off and disappeared out of sight.

Tony turned back and walked upstairs to his room. He was sleeping when Emeka came back and woke him up about 10 p.m. 'Hi, Tony, what's up? You're already sleeping, anything the matter?'

'No, brother,' he answered. 'I'm at a cross-road concerning Ugomma.' 'What about her?' Emeka enquired.

'Boy, the babe was here all through this evening. We eventually made passionate love. But my worry is that she refused my proposal with an air of finality?

'Well, not to worry or brood about it. But catch your fun while she gives it. Enjoy her and maintain a good relationship. There are other nice babes also who are longing for such offers. The problem with these babes is that enmeshed in the euphoria of university life, they mess up lifetime opportunities as they befriend sugar daddies, profligate around the cities, hope for never-would- materialise marriage proposals from Yankee Nigerians, and cast aspersion on serious suitors amongst their course mates, only for them to graduate from school faced with the realities in the macro-system, only to discover that appearance is no reality. Go to the banks and see the corporate ladies without husbands. Advertise a vacancy and count how many applicants you will receive. No human being is indispensable. Boy! Leave that thing.'

'Emeka, although I love Ugomma more than any other girl, I've just resolved to enjoy myself to the maximum and forget about the proposal. Someday, somehow, I'm going to find maybe a better babe that will appreciate and believe in me for life.'

That weekend was uneventful for Ugomma other than going to the saloon to set her hair and attending the church service with Mfon her friend at the Victory Chapel within the campus. After that, she decided to stay put in her room and study for the rest of the day. But then, she had focused her mind on seeing Stephen Daniel in Eket town, having been to the town on many occasions when she visited with Mfon.

Then came Tuesday morning. Ugomma did her morning chores briskly; she finished her toileting early enough, before the place became messed up. She did not bother to think about what dress to wear, since she had selected her latest corporate suit for the outing over the weekend. She arrived in Eket town at 10.48 a.m. and had to get into a cab at the park, which was going to Ibeno (Qua Ibeno) where the Mobil QIT was situated besides the beautiful Ibeno beach. Of course, it being her first visit to the QIT, Ugomma was captivated by the serene environment down at the shore of the beach with a well-tended grass lawn stretching farther down the sea threshold. She also observed at the security gate a lot of people wanting to enter the complex. The security personnel were not finding it funny handling the crowd simultaneously.

And to Ugomma's chagrin, the majority of the people were female students from the University of Uyo. Some of them she recognised. Moreover, she also discovered that Tuesdays and Thursdays were Mobil vendors' days. However, after thirty minutes in the waiting room, she was linked up with Daniel, who was about to leave the office for lunch break. I will be with you in five minutes' time,' he informed her. So she anxiously waited. Eventually, Daniel parked his Honda Accord car outside the gate and strolled back regally towards the crowded waiting room. Ugomma, already pissed off and anxious to leave any moment, spotted Daniel through the transparent glass widow and excused herself to go outside into the refreshing sea breeze with a sigh of relief.

Daniel stopped in his tracks as he observed the beautiful lady walking towards him, whom he recognised very well, because Ugomma had this peculiar striking facial appearance of never forget me. But what was remarkable now was that Ugomma had radically transformed into a more matured beautiful lady than the school girl he had met the previous time. 'Mr Daniel Stephen, it's nice meeting you again.'

'It's wonderful, Ugomma,' he responded. I never thought of meeting you again. You know, babes with their ways of rationality and approach think it socially wrong tracing a man whom they've only met for the first time. In fact, I'm delighted welcoming you here he said while opening the passenger door of his car for her. Slamming the door and turning round to the driver's seat, he fastened the belt and drove off into the complex proper.

As they drove down, he said, 'Ugomma, I'm sorry you visited today as it is Contractors' day. In fact, the best day to visit is on Wednesday. Nonetheless, you can always phone to confirm my whereabouts before embarking on such visits.'

'That's all right, although I wanted to know this place because I've heard a lot about here, especially concerning the beach.'

'Okay, the beach is full of great fun during the weekends. Your students are always here for picnic. Some come to celebrate birthdays,' Daniel explained.

Daniel, after showing Ugomma his office, took her to the Mobil banquet hall. 'The lunch is a buffet. Serve yourself.' Later, they returned to his office, collected his briefcase, and drove off to Eket town as he had no intention of returning to the office that day. Meanwhile, they arrived at No. 27, Oron Road, the residence of Daniel, at about 3 p.m.

'Here we are, Ugomma he announced to her as they got out from the car. He locked the car, and they climbed the staircase of the storey building block of four flats. He opened the out-burglary gate, the main wooden door, and ushered her into the living room. He flung his briefcase on the reading table and turned to face Ugomma. 'You're highly welcome to my home he said with his arms wide open to hug her. She obliged, and they warmly embraced each other. Daniel kissed her passionately, longer than Ugomma would've imagined. But she couldn't stop him. 'Please, darling, make yourself comfortable and feel at home.' Meanwhile, the buzzing air-conditioner started changing the temperature in the room, as Daniel emerged from the kitchen with two glasses and a bottle of wine, smiling at Ugomma, who responded to him. Setting those down on the table, he excused himself and strolled into his master bedroom, singing along with the soft music of Alex. O's 'My banana' that was playing in the background. Ugomma, therefore, had time to look around, and she spotted a particular picture hanging on the wall amongst others, which was of Daniel and his wife with their two children.

Then Daniel joined her in the sofa half dressed, only in his shorts. He poured out a drink into both the glasses, handed one to her, raised his cup to her, and cheered, laughing. And Ugomma commended, 'Daniel, what a nice home you have here.'

'O! Thanks, Ugomma.' While sharing their drinks, Daniel told her about his family residing at Calabar and his wife, who was a medical doctor working with the University of Calabar Teaching Hospital. And their two children Mike and Sophia were in the University of Calabar's Model Primary School. So he spent most weekends with his family at Calabar. And so he told her all about his background training abroad as an electrical electronic engineer and all about him that Ugomma needed to know. After which, Ugomma reciprocated in telling him about herself and her family background. As they spoke, Daniel drew her closer to himself and started playing and caressing the sensual parts of her body. Because of the effects of the alcohol which she had already consumed, she became tipsy and incoherent about her story in which Daniel was no more interested, as he was now busy undressing, cuddling, and kissing her. She eventually could not even remember where she left off the story. The ember of sensation burning in her became aflame when Daniel expertly thrust his finger into her vagina, rubbing the wall of her clitoris which was already erect, his mouth sucking hungrily on her scintillating tender breasts. Feeling weak as if dreaming, she started moaning softly and opened wide her long legs, inviting him in. He took her right there on the sofa. Later, he carried her into the bedroom and made love to her two more times before they had a bath together. It was the first ever Ugomma had shared a bath with any man. It was another fun, because Daniel had to bathe her practically like a baby. Eventually, ready to go, she rejected the money offered by Daniel and made him understand that she had enough and also to spare. It was about 6.30 p.m. when Daniel dropped her off at Eket motor park, with an arrangement for her to come back on Saturday and stay till Sunday as Daniel had decided not to visit his family at Calabar that weekend. Instead of boarding a bus, she got into a cab to save time. Daniel bid her goodbye and the car drove off.

Chapter Six

Ugomma got to the campus about 8 p.m., and when she entered her room, she discovered that Tony and Emeka had visited and dropped a note on her reading table. Uduak also informed her that Mfon her friend had also visited. However, she decided not going to anywhere, but she changed her clothing, lay down on the bed, and dozed off. It was around 9.20 p.m. when Mfon re-visited her but found her sleeping. She enquired from Uduak at what time Ugomma had returned and she was duly informed.

Shaking her gently, Mfon fondly called her, 'Ugo, wake up, darling. You can't be sleeping now.' Ugomma opened her eyes and looked at Mfon bending over her. She saw worry deep inside her friend's eyes and sat up, relaxing her back against the wall, holding her pillow on her lap. 'Tell me, Ugo, where've you been all day? You did not come for lectures in the morning, and after the first two lectures that ended by 12 noon, I rushed down here to find out whether you'd taken ill over the night, but couldn't find you. All through the day after lectures, this is my fourth visitation, today. You made me quite pretty worried without any prior information.'

'Don't be offended, my sweetheart,' Ugomma tried to soothe her friend. 'I actually visited my friend, Daniel Stephen, at Mobil QIT, Eket, with the intention of returning back before 3 p.m., but my dear, events overtook that proposition.'

'I see!' Mfon responded. 'You went to catch fun, abandoning you studies, while I was worried stupid for you, isn't it? Well, let me caution you while there is time. You'd better take Tony seriously and secure your future with him and adequately face your academics without distractions from men. You've started emulating the NFAs. In the end, you will be the one to tell the bitter stories.'

'Hold it, Mfon,' she ordered, flaring up. 'How dare you talk to me like that?' Mfon was shocked at Ugomma's outburst. Instead of picking a quarrel with her friend, she quietly rose up from the bed and walked out of the room.

In the days following that, Ugomma was all on her own; she tried as much as possible to avoid Mfon, both in and out of the class. Tony was not also spared. Then came Saturday, and she packed a small travelling bag with a change of clothes, including her bikini and other personal effects, and travelled to Eket. She got to Daniel's home before 10 a.m. Of course, he was expecting her and had prepared everything they would need for the beach. But since Ugomma had not eaten breakfast before leaving Uyo, she entered the kitchen to prepare fried plantain, eggs, and coffee. Daniel joined her there to show her where the things that were needed were kept. In the course of doing that, he started touching her. 'O, Dan, stop it! Just let me finish frying this dodo (plantain) so that it does not get burnt.'

'Umm! Darling,' he murmured into her right ear. I can't stop loving you as you've gate crashed into my world, and the wall of my marital vows has got cracks. Imagine me spending a weekend without my family for the first time!'

'Oh! Daniel, do you need to talk like that?' she challenged him teasingly.

'Not to worry, baby. I am going to make it up someday for my sweet Belinda.' He left her and walked back into the sitting room and put on the music of UB40 'Red Red Wine'.

It was fun time at the beach, and they had a great time. Ugomma was the cynosure of all eyes, and Daniel was proud that he had brought her along. In her bikini, Ugomma was glowing and looking beautiful. The other big boys of Mobil staff club could not hide their admiration. There were cheering accolades for Daniel, who savoured all the attention that his elegant babe was attracting from all around. Even some expatriates whistled their approval from a distance. The reflection of the rising sun transformed Ugomma into a Mexican model with the perfectly fitted sunglasses that she wore.

Although there were other students from UniUyo seeking fun around, she didn't bother herself with such frivolity—triviality of gossip. She was enjoying herself and cared less about whatever anybody thought or did about that. Howbeit, with the setting of the sun, they reluctantly packed their things and drove back to Eket town. They made a stopover at a supermarket, did some shopping, and drove home. In the evening, they occupied their time with watching the CNN World News, with the latest news splash that the United States Supreme Court had finally decided to suspend hand recounting of votes of the presidential election in the State of Florida, where the contesting candidates Vice President Al Gore and W. Bush (governor of the State of Texas) of the Republican Party were running neck to neck. It was also interesting that the younger brother of Bush was the governor of Florida State. That was why there was suspicion of foul play as there were uncounted votes allegedly belonging to Al Gore, which had been picked up from the waters of Florida. Trust the Americans; the entire security network and the general public were on red alert following the events sequentially. Remarkably, this political development was unprecedented in American history. A school of thought postulated that this development had brought a biblical and spiritual undertone, linking the Nebuchadnezzar vision in the Book of Daniel, depicting end-time. The outgoing distinguished beloved president of the United States of America, the friend of Africa, Jefferson Bill Clinton, had been briefed about this latest development following which he phoned his vice president from Northern Ireland, where he was brokering a Peace Accord with Tony Blair and other European leaders. Therefore, the stalemate political impasse of the U.S. election, which held the entire world spellbound, had been resolved in Bush's favour.

'Hi, Ugomma, do you see that history has a way of repeating itself?' Daniel commented as they played chess. 'Honestly, the intricacies of politics can only be understood from the strict adherents to the tenets and principle of the law. If not for the belief, trust, and confidence the American people have in their judicial system, this episode is capable of rocking their beautiful democracy as a world paradigm. My dear, I hope someday Nigeria will get there said Daniel.

'Sure, I do believe, only if we become sincere to ourselves and not this attitude of "who is fooling who nationality and ethnocentrism".'

They unavoidably made love several times before daybreak. But the part that Ugomma enjoyed the most was during the early morning from 4 to 5 a.m., when the dawn light appeared on the horizon. It gave her humid sleeping soul refreshment and activation for the busy day ahead. The libido in Ugomma together with her juvenile ebullience craved for more, and it seemed she never could get enough. She woke thereafter, boiled coffee, and served them both on bed, knowing, they couldn't muster courage to attend Church service that morning. Ugomma did his laundry, cooked, and tidied up the whole apartment. They wasted the remaining day in all there was about sex. They showered together, ate, and slept off into fairy-land, only for them to wake up around 6 p.m.

'Daniel she called out to him, 'I'm ready to go.'

'Yea, baby, am going to drive you back to the campus. I can't afford to let you use public transport after all the unreserved swell time you provided for the weekend.'

'O darling! I appreciate it.'

'One more thing, Ugo beauty. From now on, you don't need to travel back to Lagos through Calabar. You can use the Mobil airstrip here in Eket, off this Oron Road, because it's faster and more comfortable.' Ugomma responded by flinging herself at him and hugging him with passionate kisses.

They arrived at the UniUyo annex campus at 8 p.m. Daniel parked his car in front of Ugomma's hostel; they came out of the car after he engaged the security device in the car and locked up, and they walked into her room. Usually, in this period of the evening, lots of cars thronged the hostel environs. Men of all status came in to check on their girlfriends, who were referred to as oppressors, customers, in-laws by the male students. Sunday evenings were usually the peak of visiting activities in the female hostels of both campuses. So it was then when Ugomma and her friend Daniel stepped into her room. There was a momentary silence from the room-mates. Some were perplexed and derisive, while some of her room-mates, especially Ogechi and Onome, became green. The two were the first to greet Ugomma and her visitor gluttonously. Circumstance had made the oil-workers in Nigeria a kind of special breed, in that they were well fed and cared for. Hence, it was very easy to distinguish Daniel as a successful young man. Ugomma's profile no doubt had assumed a large status with this visit.

Therefore, she did not bother to introduce Daniel based on his instruction. Probably he was trying to hide his identity and avoid giving some of those girls a lead or clue so that they would not come in to trace him at Mobil with their pestering. This indulgence Daniel knew from his previous observation and experience at workplace. Eventually, after staying awhile, he decided to depart. Ugomma, therefore, proudly saw him off to the car. And he drove away into the cloud of the night.

With time in the next few weeks, Ugomma acquired the status of 'one of the happening babes on campus', to the detriment of her studies. Looking good and feeling good became the top priority of Ugomma, as if that was the main objective that had brought her to the university. She walked regally, sometimes sauntering in the evenings around the hostel environments, attracting unnecessary attention to herself. Most provoking was the way she rolled her rounded buttocks and the rhythmic heaving of her matured breasts while walking. The guys kept turning around in their strides. But the girls discussed her with jealousy.

It got to a climax as young men lecturers desired to get her laid. Hence, they plotted to trap her in any event she failed their courses. Apparently, she observed a lot and kept her ears to the ground through the hostel's porters, whom she had influenced by her generosity. Thereby, she stayed clear of troubled waters before the turbulent sea rolled. Obstinately, Ugomma attended classes at will and late too. She would come into the class when lectures were midway gone and reclined in the very background where the NFAs normally stayed, as back-benchers. But alas, Mfon was weeping inside and at crossroads on how to help resuscitate Ugomma's confidence and trust, which she had lost while trying to caution her the other time. That incident had strained their relationship, affecting Tony also, who would always plead with Mfon to know what had gone wrong with Ugomma and probably reconcile issues. Obviously, Ugomma had become more arrogant than nature had bequeathed to her loving soul. Mfon meditated upon all this day and night, but committed Ugomma to prayers.

Six weeks later, Ugomma started feeling weak, intermittently drowsy, and funny inside her stomach, especially the lower abdominal region. That Wednesday morning, as usual, she packed a few items into her handbag and zoomed off to Eket. Getting there almost at the verge of lunch time, she easily passed the security point and entered Daniel's office. Luckily enough he was in and less busy. After explaining her condition to him, they had lunch at the staff banquet and left for Eket town. On reaching there, Daniel took her to his friend, a medical doctor at Grace-Land specialist hospital that was equipped with a contemporary laboratory. They ran a test for her blood and other processes within forty-five minutes while they waited. The result was shockingly positive, confirming her fear.

The compelling reality was excruciating for Ugomma, as if the world had collapsed on her shoulders. Invariably, she fainted in the consulting room of the doctor. Daniel was thrown into panic and utter confusion, but it was the doctor who expertly brought the scenario under control. Ugomma was perfectly revived, but she looked downcast, drained, and stupefied with many thoughts running amok in her fickle mind. The million-dollar question that refused to be voiced out by the incriminated duo was: What to do with the unwanted pregnancy?

Daniel dared not think of adopting the pregnancy because he wouldn't allow anything in the world snag his relationship with his adoring wife and beautiful children. Neither would Ugomma in her wildest dream think of carrying an unwanted pregnancy around the campus. Her ostrich pride was punctured hollow. Her parents would almost die of shame and really disown her. All the advice and hope of her beloved family flashed as a memory before her, and she broke down pitiably and wept profusely which moved Daniel and the doctor. 'I'm sorry Ugo darling said Daniel. 'In this unfortunate precarious circumstance, the only option we do have left is abortion. The doctor can conveniently handle that Dr Japheth responded cordially to Daniel's suggestion. Ugomma surprised the two men by instantaneously wiping off her tears with the back of her left hand and stoically announced her readiness to comply with the doctor. Still enmeshed in wonderment and lost for words, Daniel looked strongly at his friend, who nudged him on to excuse them. Daniel stepped out of the room.

The doctor concluded the abortion process within twenty minutes. The dastardly act was however recorded by nature for her. Daniel took her home, and she was seriously weary and devastated in mind and body to venture going back to the university, which would be suicidal to her personality, pride, and composure. She needed time to cool off and regain her composure and confidence before returning to campus. Daniel had no problem in allowing her to stay till the weekend.

Invariably, Ugomma stayed indoors all through the days, watching television, eating, and sleeping. Her conscience had been bruised; she often brooded deeply, but she knew she had to brace up or else she could cause more harm to herself. Hence, she resolved as quickly as possible as reality had compelled her to understand and accept factually that she had no part with Daniel and did not belong to his world. It was only foolishness that could make her perverse, for her drowning soul still believed in him.

Consequently, by Saturday afternoon, she decided to return to campus while Daniel prepared to travel to Calabar to visit his family. But before their departure, as Ugomma was taking her bath, Daniel hid 500 pieces of the new crisp N200.00 notes gummed together, amounting to 20,000 naira, in the corner of Ugomma's bag because she had rejected to accept any monetary gifts or gratification from any person. Her father was a multimillionaire and generously spared out to his children. Just two weeks ago, he had transferred 50,000 naira into her account in Eu-reka International Bank. Therefore, on reaching Uyo that afternoon, Daniel dropped her off at Ikpa-Ikot Ekpene Road junction, close to the university gate. He gave her a mild kiss before she hopped out, closed the door, and bid him goodbye. Daniel drove away to Calabar. Ugomma flagged down a motorcyclist and rode down Ikpa Road to the annex campus gate. While she was strolling innocently to her hostel, Mfon who was stepping out of her hostel at that instance saw Ugomma and couldn't refrain herself from running up to her because she loved her with all her soul and regarded her as a blood sister. Ugomma heard running steps towards her direction and turned sharply. 'Ugo darling, I terribly missed you. Please, where've you been?'

Ugomma now in the light of her horrifying experience had become more sober than ever before. She hugged Mfon, then responded by holding her hands and leading the way to her hall and room.

While the other room-mates were sleeping, Yetunde and Fatima, her old-cum-new room-mates, welcomed Ugomma and faithful Mfon into the room. Obviously, by now Ugomma had not only recuperated but also radiated the same old composure and confidence. This was the charisma that made her endearing to people. Without much ado, Ugomma and Mfon reconciled without any reference to the past. Mfon gave her progress reports about all academics and that Tony and Emeka were all longing to see her again. They had also started tutorials in virtually all the courses, as exams were just one week away to commence. They stayed together till late. At 7.35 p.m., they both went to Mfon's room, where she had not been to for quite some time.

No wonder Mfon's room-mates were excited on seeing her again and warmly welcomed her. Instead of going out for dinner, they decided to use Mfon's boiling ring to cook Indomie noodles with eggs. They ate their dinner and gist heartily.

The next day was Sunday. Ugomma couldn't attend church service; rather, she busied herself with laundering and putting her bedside corner in shape, which had been neglected because of her long absence. In the process, she found Tony's note that he'd written during her absence. After reading it, she tore it into shreds and cast the pieces into a waste bin. She also discovered the money Daniel had inserted in her handbag and frowned displeasingly; she closed the bag and put it away inside the wardrobe.

In contrast, exams actually commenced the next week as given in the exams time table. Ugomma was caught napping as she had virtually whiled away precious time chasing after vain shadows throughout most of the outgoing semester. She expectedly found the question papers intriguing and confusing because she had never attended classes or prepared adequately for the exams. The same day she wrote her last paper she exchanged pleasantries with Mfon and flew back to Lagos.

Chapter Seven

The events of the ouster semester had created a great vacuum in Ugomma's life, which constantly beclouded her thoughts and beat her imaginations hollow. From where should she start to pick the pieces of her shattered aspirations? Was it the family's hope on her education, even if the financial expenditure so far could be insignificant considering her family background? The worst thing that plagued her joy and peace of mind was the memory of that abortion she had committed. So, all through the holidays, she put up a facade in front of her mother. Of course, now that she was more mature and exposed, she could successfully manoeuvre and aptly control her emotions, no matter the mood and prevailing circumstance. Thereby, she could keep her own secrets and let go only those information she considered not hurtful to her person. Her indulgence in falsehood had been established because *sin is a linkage,* especially when human ego is at stake. She made her parents believe there was nothing wrong with her educational pursuits. Well, they actually had no choice but accept her stories because they had been preoccupied in recent times in their business, making money and globe-trotting, expanding the strategies of their influential empire.

So it was after having a swell time during the Xmas and New Year holidays that Ugomma arrived back at the campus with special resolutions to become more serious with her studies, with the view of amending the disaster that was the last semester. Also, she wanted to reconcile with Tony, with the hope of actually negotiating for his apartment and packing out of the hostel which she now considered disgusting. By 22 January in the New Year, most students had returned to the campus, bearing in mind how short but cumbersome was the second semester with lots of activities. And so did the final year students, who were at the threshold of graduation; hence, some actually did not travel for the holiday per se, but organised funds and rushed back to the campus. Quite a lot arrived earlier with the intention to find out the possibility of sorting the lecturers and better their results in courses of deficiencies. The political jugglers for the student union government elections were not left out. By and large, the socio-political activities of the second semester could be an illusion, the nimbus of the skies for the unfocussed students. This was university. The milling system of enculturation depended on what any individual chose to become at the end of the procession.

'Hi, Ugomma, you are welcome back. How was your family?' the porter on duty greeted her, as she rushed up to assist Ugomma in carrying one of her luggage, as she disembarked from the taxi in front of her hostel. Young teenagers of the locality did brisk business during closing or resumption times like this, doing manual jobs and eking out a living; babes were usually their targets, so they scrambled for Ugomma's luggage.

'Anty, welcome and happy new year they greeted her.

'Thank you, young folks, and happy new year also she responded. 'Ah! Ekaette, happy new year to you 0 Ugomma greeted the porter. Together they entered her room and met Mercy, who had also returned earlier that afternoon. Ugomma, being generous as ever, dispatched the young stars with a gift of 100 naira a piece and also gave Ekaette a 200 naira note. Joyfully, they ran away expectantly for the next arrivals, while she busied herself settling down.

'Compliments to you, Ugomma Mercy greeted her.

'The same to you, my sister. It's a pleasure coming back to where we belong Ugomma responded.

'You arrived earlier this time around Mercy interjected.

'Sure, I got to tidy up things and settle down fast before academics starts Ugomma replied while unpacking her belongings and stacking things in the proper places, listening to a classical jazz blaring from her musical set. Being highly domesticated, within a short time Ugomma had accomplished in putting things in their right places. As usual, she had brought in new things; every semester, she changed her wardrobe, bedding accessories, etc. Hence, with lots of can juice and drinks that she had brought down from Lagos, she prepared food for herself and Mercy and stocked the remaining canned food in the cupboard. Thereafter, she washed and cleaned up the place and relaxed on her bed with a novel to read in leisure. That evening, all her room-mates also arrived, and it was a happy reunion as well as an exchange of pleasantries all through.

Intuitively, Ugomma has been expecting Tony and was not surprised when there was a knock at the door, and he entered the room looking handsome, very healthy, and well kept. Invariably, he stretched out his hands for a shake, but Ugomma surprised him with a warm hug and kissed him without blushing even though her room-mates were looking. They laughed hilariously at the duo, especially at Ugomma's innocent child-like excitement. Ugomma dragged him playfully to her corner, and they sat down smiling at each other. Meanwhile, many pieces of a puzzle were filtering in Tony's mind. He didn't seem to actually understand this ambivalent ambience called Ugomma. But one basic feature that he was convinced about her was that she was resolute and did things her own way without giving a damn as to whatever anyone thought. If he was amazed the way she welcomed him, then he hadn't seen anything yet. She pulled out a small travelling bag and handed it over to him.

'What do I do with it?' Tony demanded.

'That question is not necessary. The bag is for you. But please don't open it here until you arrive back home.' He obliged, and they gist till 8.45 p.m., when Tony decided to leave.

'Ugomma, when are you visiting me?' Tony asked, thinking that she would respond negatively.

'Tony darling, tomorrow will be okay, say around 2 p.m.?' She eventually escorted him to the annex gate. Tony called an okada, then kissed her, and the cyclist drove off into the distant night. Ugomma, pleased with herself on having solved one major nagging problem, returned to her room.

Tony got to his room, bemused; he anxiously opened the bag and discovered its contents: a pair of fine Italy maroon shoes, designer trousers, and two shirts to match, as well as underwear and fifty crisp 200 naira notes, amounting to 10,000 naira only. It became mixed grill for him. Doubts and excitement clouded his mind. What's she up to? But as he was admiring the shoes, a paper fell out from the right leg; it was a short note neatly written in Ugomma's handwriting, which read thus:

> Tony dear,
> I don't mean to bruise your manly ego. I sincerely care and wish to share. Thanks for understanding me.
> Ugomma

He read the note over and over again before going to sleep that night, and he accepted the obvious with reference to his last semester's resolve of enjoying the goodies of their relationship while it lasted.

Consequently, at the exact time as proposed, Ugomma knocked at the door. Earlier in the morning hours, he had finished runs for the day for his project supervisor, Dr A. Ikpe, to finally vet his work and now had given it out for typesetting to be done on computer. So he was indoors, waiting for Ugomma. 'Come in,' he responded to the visitor who happened to be Ugomma. He hugged and kissed her welcome. She sat down beside him on the bed, sipping the drink he offered her. Understandably, she was patiently waiting for Tony to bring up the gift issue for discussion. 'Ugomma! The content of that bag is quite a surprise, although your note explained your feeling. But can you expatiate on that?' he asked.

'Well, Tony, I'm not a stranger to you and vice versa. But I'll appreciate you let things be the way they are, okay?' she pleaded.

'That's all right, Ugomma.'

She then asked about Emeka, and Tony informed her that Dr Eminue Okon, the head of the department, who was Emeka's project supervisor, had given the final approval for his work. Invariably, he had travelled to Owerri to see his folks and would be back next Tuesday morning. 'And what about last semester's exams? I hope you fared well,' he asked her. Although the entire last semester had been like a bad dream, the dark age of Ugomma's life, yet she couldn't tell Tony about it and wished that that page of her university experience could be closed forever. So she lied to Tony and fed him with hopeful information. Like a recurring decimal, their bodies that had been touching started passing electrifying currents and messages to their brains, which Tony's hand communicated with actions. Ugomma had now more exposure and was experienced about men and understood the signals, but she could not stop what was coming. Even if her spirit could, her emotions betrayed her with swift responses. However, she managed to stop Tony before the real act; she pulled out her own condom and inserted into her vagina before allowing him to make love to her. This also surprised Tony. But once beaten, twice shy, Ugomma had learnt the bitter lesson of growing up. Never again would any man have sex with her without a condom, not even on the flimsy excuse of not having one ready. So she carried a packet in her bag whenever she had a date or was casually visiting any man. Hence, you men, don't be amazed when a lady vehemently doesn't allow you to look into their little mobile warehouse, as they don't want you to regard them as being promiscuous.

Their stay together was worthwhile, and she departed around 6 p.m. back to the campus. She arrived to find Mfon's note waiting for her, informing her of her return to the campus at about 4 p.m. and requesting her to come over immediately she came back from wherever. Hence, Ugomma went right away to look for Mfon in her hall. Howbeit, Mfon was sleeping when Ugomma entered her room. But she had to wake her up. 'Bless my soul! Ugomma, where have you been? I've been lonely and needed your company.'

'Not to worry, darling. I was visiting with Tony since the afternoon. And how are things with you, the family, and the holidays?'

'Not bad at all, only I missed you,' answered Mfon. They gist till well into the evening and had dinner together, which Mfon cooked in her room.

Three weeks after resumption, the results of the penultimate semester were published, and Ugomma was the worst for it. She failed in all her courses. 'Ugomma, you're looking so dejected,' observed Mfon. 'What's the matter with you?'

'Mfon, do you mean that you've not seen the last semester results published this afternoon?' she replied to her friend Mfon.

'No! And what are they like that should affect you so deeply?'

'My dear, I'm finished' was Ugomma's final answer as she could not hold back the tears falling from her eyes. Though Mfon had envisaged some failures, because of Ugomma's truancy in the past semester, she had not expected this kind of outright failure in all the courses. That unavoidably spelled doom for Ugomma's career.

'Look, Ugomma, let's get out of here. Our course mates are wondering what the problem is with you.'

'Oh! Mfon, I'm in trouble.'

'Take it easy, Ugomma. This is not the end of life, although definitely your career is at stake said Mfon consolingly.

As they walked away from their departmental block towards the hostel area, Ugomma changed her mind about going into the hall and branched off to the garden beside the faculty block. 'Mfon! What am I going to do now?' Ugomma asked her friend.

'That means that in year three, first semester, instead of registering for new courses, you've to repeat all the year two first semester courses and probably one or two new courses as allowed by the faculty. Invariably, you're not graduating with the rest of the members of our course mates,' Mfon explained pitiably. Now alone with Mfon in the garden, Ugomma wept bitterly about the mess she had made of her academics. Obviously, the situation was irreparable as they both evaluated all alternatives and came to the conclusion that Ugomma should hang on faith while doomsday waited.

In the weeks ahead, Ugomma could not find her bearing any more. Awareness is a mental process that changes the behaviour and character and empowers the individual. This empowerment depends on the qualitative education imbibed, which should foster the frontiers of knowledge, and optimum utilisation of such knowledge by the individual facilitates achieving the set objectives so that the entire efforts do not end up in utter futility.

Days later, Mfon observed, 'Ugomma, you've been brooding and probably not eating well. I didn't see you in the class today, and that's why I decided to rush down here as soon as the last lecture was over this afternoon.'

'Mfon, my sister, thanks for caring, and thank goodness that you're here. All through the night, I've not been feeling fine. Even after taking Panadol-extra, I still feel this nagging headache that has refused to subside.'

'Why, let's visit the medical centre,' suggested Mfon.

'That should be all right,' Ugomma agreed. So she got dressed, and both of them walked out of the hostel to the campus gate and flagged down a motorcyclist who drove them straight to the medical centre. Eventually, they met with Dr S. Uwem Ekanem, an amiable, caring young woman, who was known among the students for her kindness.

'Good afternoon, Doctor,' the duo greeted her.

'Good afternoon, my young ladies, may I know the problem?' she asked them.

'Please, Doctor, my friend Ugomma is having a nagging headache since the night and the energetic tablets so far taken could not relieve her.'

'I see she responded. Well, after observing her temperature and other diagnosis, she psychologically discovered through the probing questions that she asked Ugomma that her problem was just hard thinking and lack of adequate rest. And because she was down to earth and loving, Ugomma confided in her about the source of her worry. She counselled her, 'Look, my dear, you've to work hard because failure and success have no alibis.' She finally prescribed some drugs for her. Mfon and Ugomma left feeling better. Things would never be the same again because the harm had already been done. And it was terrible at that, but life went on for Ugomma, who now knew that her days as a law three student in the university were numbered. Although she worked harder, her rustication from the faculty was imminent, and what next?

Then came the student union week in mid-May, and Ugomma was in a dire need of change in environment, at least to ease off the accumulated tension and stress in her life. She didn't want to go back home to Lagos, nor visit her maternal uncle in Port Harcourt. These aforementioned places would expose her present circumstances. She was in this dilemma when Fatima Yusuf, her room-mate and friend, mentioned about visiting her folks at Jos, Plateau State, in two days time. 'Hi, Ugomma, I intend travelling to Jos during this student union week and hope to be back by Sunday next week.'

'Really? I would love to join you, as my first ever visit to the north. I hope there are interesting places there?' Ugomma asked.

'Yes, of course, you should know that Jos is the foremost city of film industry in Nigeria, with lots of natural settings like rocky plateau highlands that secures the city, like the mount Zion. Talking more of the climatic conditions, it's just wonderful. In fact, about five kilometres away from the city, you will observe and feel the changes in the atmosphere. A cool breeze will cuddle your soul to solace. And that is why you have lots of white people residing and visiting there all year round because Jos is the only city in the entire West Africa with the same climate as the temperate regions of the world.'

'O! That's beautiful,' responded Ugomma. 'At least, let me use this opportunity to visit there. And I prefer that we travel by road to enable me see and appreciate the vastness of this great country.'

'That's all right,' replied Fatima. 'You'll surely enjoy the excursion.' That evening, there was a torrential thunderstorm which preceded serious floods everywhere. Hence, no one bothered going outside; neither Mfon nor Ugomma could reach each other till the next day.

In the morning, Ugomma cheerfully visited her beloved friend, Mfon, to inform her about the latest arrangement of travelling to Jos with Fatima. 'Hi, Mfon, fine morning to you.'

'Hello, Ugomma, my sister, how was your night, and how do you feel now?'

'I'm fine,' replied Ugomma.

'I can see you're more cheerful this morning. Is it the rainfall of last night that has watered your soul?' Mfon asked.

'Well, dear, you can say that again! The fact is that I and Fatima have arranged to travel to Jos tomorrow.'

'Yes, Ugomma, I think that this trip will be good for you, as a change of environment at this time will help to soothe the frayed nerves and rejuvenate your unfocussed mind. But when are you supposed to come back?' Mfon asked.

'Well, Fatima talked of returning Sunday next week,' answered Ugomma.

'That means you girls intend to spend the entire student union week out there in Jos?'

'Something like that,' answered Ugomma.

'Okay, I wish you two a safe trip.'

'Thanks, Mfon, but please do inform Tony about this development and that I hope seeing him when I come back, especially concerning meeting his landlord about the apartment as we discussed sometime ago. So long, Mfon!'

'And you too responded Mfon, as Ugomma walked away.

At 7.45 a.m. on 20 May, Thursday, at the Young Shall Grow Transport Company garage on Abak Road, Fatima and Ugomma purchased their tickets and boarded the luxurious bus; fifteen minutes later, after all the passengers had boarded, the driver engaged the engine and horned sportingly before driving the vehicle out of the garage.

At Itam junction, the driver decided to follow the Itu Road to take the Odukpani-Calabar Ogoja route instead of the Aba-0 werri-Onitsha-Auchi-Abuja route. 'Fatima, do you observe that there are lots of rubber plantations along this Odukpani-Ogoja axis?' Ugomma asked.

'Yes, Ugomma, you'll also see that the vegetation, which is thickly forested here in the south, will start to sparse out the moment we enter the middle-belt regions said Fatima. Invariably, in the course of the journey, the driver made a stopover at Ogoja, where there were cottage industries and cattle ranches like Houston and Boston of Texas. The passengers at this juncture were supposed to freshen themselves and probably have their breakfast before continuing their journey.

'Ugomma, let's go and eat food at that cafe down there,' said Fatima.

'But will there be enough time for us to eat? Shouldn't we just buy snacks which we can even eat inside the bus?' Ugomma asked.

'Don't bother about time. Even the driver and his bus conductor are gone in there to eat also,' observed Fatima.

'That's all right then. Let's go,' responded Ugomma. After their meal, they were accosted by a woman selling fruits. 'Hi, Fatima, can you imagine the size of these mangoes. It's just as big as a child's head. You mean there's this kind of wonder yields in this country?' Ugomma asked.

'Ah! Ugo, you've not seen anything yet. Wait till we reach Jos. Not only this kind of big mangoes, but you'll be excited seeing varieties of fresh vegetables and sweet Irish potatoes,' said Fatima. They all boarded the bus and continued their journey, more relaxed now. As they were crossing the bridge of river Benue, behind it was Makurdi town, and further down the river was the place where Rivers Niger and Benue met. Ugomma became more adventurous and jotted down sketches and names of the places that interested her. At 2 p.m., they got to Lokoja town, the capital of Kogi State. Eventually, they also got to Abuja by 4 p.m.

'Fatima, I suppose here is Abuja.'

'Yes, it is, Ugomma.'

'*Wa-wao!* Fatima, this city is beautiful and well planned. The road network is superb,' observed Ugomma. I remember that Abuja officially assumed the status of capital city of the Federal Republic of Nigeria on 12 December 1992, under the military regime of General Ibrahim B. Babaginda.' Through the Nya-nya-Laffia Road, they proceeded up to Keffi. 'Fatima.'

'Yes, Ugo,' she responded, now fully awake.

'Where're we now?' Ugomma asked.

'This place is called Jaji, where you have the school of Strategic and Policy Studies of the Federal Government of Nigeria. In fact, all the military top brass in the Armed Forces of Nigeria at one time or the other passed through the institution.'

'Really?' responded Ugomma.

'Ah! My friend, you're already getting cold,' observed Fatima.

'Fatima, this journey's very far O! When are we arriving at Jos?' asked Ugomma, who was now tired of the trip.

'Not to worry, my dear. In the next ten to twenty minutes, we should be getting into the city of Jos,' replied Fatima.

In the next fifteen minutes, the entire atmosphere changed, and it was five kilometres to Jos. Fatima also pulled out her cardigan and wore it. That's when Ugomma remembered what Fatima said about the coldness of the city and that in a little while they would enter the city. Hence, she became really expectant. After a little more time, they approached the gate of the city, which had a bold inscription of 'Welcome to Jos, the Tin City'. And Fatima turned on her side to face Ugomma and warmly cheered to her, 'Ugomma, welcome to my place of birth, the land where my placenta of life dropped and gave me a leverage to longevity.'

'Oh thank you, Fatima, for this opportunity to come up north. I hope to enjoy the short stay,' said Ugomma.

'Definitely you will,' responded Fatima.

Subsequently, they disembarked from the bus at the transport company's park at Jos Central Terminus and picked up a taxi to drive to Yusuf's compound along Muritala Mohammed way.

There was almost fanfare with regard to the rousing welcome that was accorded to Fatima and her friend Ugomma. The show of hospitality showered on Ugomma by the Yusufs was unimaginable. The children in the compound fell in love with Ugomma instantly and nicknamed her 'Bature' because of her complexion and smashing beauty. The love, serenity, and hospitality blending around Ugomma purged her soul of the bitter anguish that had compelled her to run away from the campus.

On Friday, 21 May, the next day after they arrived, they arranged to go sightseeing. 'Ugomma, come and have your bath Fatima called.

In the bathroom, Ugomma observed that the hot water was steaming. 'Fati, the water's very hot.'

'Ugo dear, I should've informed you earlier. Look, Ugo, if you wait the next two minutes the water will freeze to the point you cannot even put your hand inside it. So go ahead and use it immediately.' Ugomma obliged. And after taking their breakfast and dressing up, Fatima lent a winter jacket to Ugomma, and they decided to go to the town. 'Daddy!'

'Yes, my daughter, Fatima.'

'I'm taking my friend out to show her some places of interest in the city.'

'That's okay, but don't stay away too long, considering the cool weather, especially for your friend who's not used to the environment,' advised Mr Yusuf.

'Okay, Dad. I've taken care of that, and I hope we should be back on time before lunch.'

'My daughters have a nice day.'

'Ugomma, come on, let's go. I think our first port of call will be the University of Jos that is situated along Jos-Zaria Road. After paying a visit to my cousin, Miriam, in Literary and Foreign Languages Department, then we'll move on to the zoo.'

'That's all right, Fati.' And they stepped out. Ugomma was wearing a blue jeans trouser and sports canvas shoes, along with a T-shirt inside a cardigan under the jacket. She had neatly knotted her long hair at the back of her head. With sunglasses and a handbag, she presented the picture of a foreign tourist on excursion in the city. 'Hi, Fatima, let's inform your parents about our movement.'

'Don't worry, Ugo. I've already informed my father. However, my mother's already gone to her shop at the Jos Central Market.'

'Okay, you mean that ultra-modern market we passed yesterday on getting to the city?'

'Yes, Ugomma,' responded Fatima.

Out on the street, on seeing them a taxi driver immediately pulled up, smiling. 'Hi, sweet ladies, I am at your service. Where do we go?' he enquired.

'Unijos campus, and how much is your charge?' Fatima asked.

'150 naira,' responded the driver.

'No, we will pay just 100 naira,' replied Fatima.

'That is okay. Come in,' said the driver.

Ugomma was delightfully surprised—not only at the cheap transport fare, but more so at the polished and polite mannerism of the driver. As both ladies sat in the back seats gossiping together, Ugo said, 'Fati, the taxi fare's very cheap here, and I'm impressed with the mannerism of this driver.'

'Oh, Ugo darling, you should've known that these drivers here over the years have garnered a wealth of experience dealing with foreign tourists that come here well often. Moreover, you easily pass as one of them and I as your guide. That's why he charged us more. Otherwise, the normal fare would've been fifty or seventy naira at the most. As for mannerisms, well, plateau people are peace loving, just like the Igbos in Diaspora. Stories have it that they have affiliation with the Igbo people. So they are also enterprising and well travelled too.

'I think that explains the stories that my father told me some time ago that it was only in Jos that the Igbos were not touched during the massacre in the north preceding the *Biafra-Nigeria* civil war,' said Ugomma.

'Yes, Ugo, my father also told me such a story,' agreed Fatima.

Just then, the driver horned and pulled out of the road, stopping in front of the gate of the University of Jos, and the ladies came out of the car. 'Here's your money, sir,' said Fatima, stretching out a 100 naira note to him.

'O, thanks, sweetheart,' replied the driver jokingly. As the duo turned and walked in through the pedestrian gate of the campus, towards the Faculty of Arts, guys stopped in their tracks, feigning to have forgotten something. Then they turned and walked past Ugomma and Fatima at a faster pace only to turn back again in the opposite direction, just to catch a full glance of these intruders in their campus. The NFAs knew regular faces on the campus and could easily identify strangers. This was not the month of October, whereby Ugomma could have been assumed as a fresher. Her snazzy and regal movements were so deliberate for a newcomer. She was a kind of lady so distinguished that you could easily pick her out of thousands. 'So who is this babe?' That was the inquisition of the guys around. One NFA guy even decided to trail them, unnoticed. But fortunately as Fatima and Ugomma approached the Literature and Foreign Languages Department, they saw Miriam and her course mate walking towards them.

'Ah! Fatima, what are you doing around here?' exclaimed Miriam as they both ran into the warm embrace of each other. 'You didn't even bother to inform me that you were coming home. Who is this epitome of beauty with you?' Miriam asked.

'Oh sure! Meet my beloved friend, Princess Ugomma, and Ugo, meet my cousin Miriam.' They both shook hands, and Fatima informed Miriam why they were visiting and when they hoped to return to Uyo.

'Ugomma, you are welcome to the Tin City. I wish I'll get a chance to draw your painting.'

'Ah! Really? You mean you can draw?'

'Sure, I'm gifted. Maybe before you both go back, say Sunday afternoon. I'll come over to the house with some art materials and you will pose for me. Within one hour, I will finish the work,' said Miriam.

'That's great!' Ugomma responded. 'I'm looking forward to that day. Make sure you keep the promise, please?

'That's all right, Ugomma! You've got yourself a date.'

'Okay, Miriam, see you on Sunday,' said Fatima, as Miriam turned to join her course mate waiting for her under an umbrella tree. And Ugomma and Fatima turned away, strolling towards the gate through which they had come. The NFA guy that had being trailing them courageously walked up to them with a smiling face and greeted them.

'Hello, fine babes, my name is Maman Dogonaro?

*1 see responded Fatima, who had previously observed him but had decided to keep quiet so as to not alert Ugomma, whose presence was wreaking a lot of attraction from the guys around there. 'Yes, my dear, what can we do for you?' Fatima asked.

'I just want to know you babes and probably be your friend replied Maman.

'Well, there is no harm in that replied Fatima, 'but the prevailing circumstances right now do not avail such an exchange of pleasantries. So do give us a break if you don't mind, and so long, sir.' Maman of course was bemused and stopped in his tracks, involuntarily waving at them as a little boy would do to his elder sisters going on a voyage.

Out of his earshot, outside the gate, Ugomma laughed and gave Fatima a pat on the back, saying, 'Kudos to a great Tusker.' Hilariously, they shook each other's hands. 'Fatima!'

'Yes, Ugo dear.'

'You wonderfully handled him. Do you know that that guy started trailing us the moment we entered that gate?'

'You mean you noticed him?' Fatima asked.

'Why not? Otherwise I'm not a great Tusker from the Ivory Republic of the University of Uyo?

'That's my darling responded Fatima as a taxi pulled up and horned to them.

'Hi, ladies, where to?'

And Fatima responded, 'To the zoo. Can you take us there?'

'With a good pay, why not? I'm at your service. I even consider it an honour to drive you babes there,' replied the taxi driver. Howbeit, they reached a bargain of 200 naira only. And as they entered the 505 Peugeot saloon car, the driver moved the car further and accelerated towards Bauchi Road, a suburb of the City. Getting to the gate of the zoo, they paid off the driver and walked down the granite-coated road leading into the complex. After the formalities at the gate, a security guard was assigned to guide them through.

The chuckling and bellowing of the animal kingdom in their natural habitat was really thrilling to Ugomma, who was seeing them alive for the first time. The monkeys, chimpanzees, gorillas, reptiles, crocodiles, pythons, and crawling creatures were in their zones. They observed the lions at a remarkable distance lying down in their domain. As they were still moving round, Ugomma started to feel uncomfortable with her breathing; the cold was really getting to her. She requested that they call it off and return to the city. And as they were retracing their way back, she heard a bird singing melodiously at the top of a tree, as if responding to the gentle breeze blowing; the shaking trees waved their leaves as if bidding Ugomma and Fatima goodbye. At the exit gate, Ugomma gave the security man a 200 naira note as a parting gift, and he thanked them happily. They crossed the road over to an art shop to buy some artefacts, which Ugomma intended to give her friends at school as souvenirs. That done, they flagged down a taxi and headed back to the city centre.

'Fatima.'

'Yes, dear.'

'I'm in love with this city. Things are at peace with nature here. Despite the Western influence over the years pertaining to the tourist attraction, the natives are proud of their cultural heritage and would not want that polluted by whatever subtle manipulations or religion.'

'Ugomma, you are right in your observation. Plateau State is actually secular in disposition, which enables many ethnic groups here the needed freedom to live harmoniously with their neighbours.'

Arriving home a little after 4 p.m., they entered the compound to the rousing welcome of the children who were waiting; they had become fond of Ugomma. 'Ah! Welcome, sisters, what did you buy for us?' the children demanded.

'Fatima, that's true. We forgot to buy something for these young stars. Well, children, go and buy something nice for yourselves, okay?!' Ugomma said while giving the eldest one among them a 100 naira note.

'*Habal* Ugo, that's much. Fifty naira would have been okay,' protested Fatima. But Ugomma firmly asserted on giving them what she had given them. 'Well, thanks all the same for being generous.'

That evening, Ugomma started coughing profusely and felt miserable with pain in her lungs, which made her breathing very difficult. Mr and Mrs Yusuf, therefore, decided to take her to the Nigerian Air Force Specialist Hospital. Fatima sat with Ugomma in the back seat while Mr and Mrs Yusuf were in the front, looking pale. Because of the incessant coughing and difficulty in breathing, Ugomma looked miserable. She leant on her friend Fatima, who was holding her pitiably, consoling her. 'Take it easy, Ugo. You'll soon be all right.'

Even though Fatima suspected that this ailment could be pneumonia, she dared not mention it so that Ugomma would not compound the problem by panicking. They got to the hospital on the Airport Road in Jos, and Mr Yusuf parked his 504 Peugeot saloon car in the parking lot, then supporting Ugomma, they walked into the hospital complex. There on duty that evening, at 6.15 p.m., were Nursing Sisters A. B. Chung and the indefatigable Christabell Ebelebe to receive Ugomma. Armed with years of experience, the duo right on the spot knew what was wrong with Ugomma, and after preliminarily taking the temperature and blood examinations, they referred her to the medical doctor as an emergency case. After the diagnosis, Dr Beutrus put Ugomma in admission till she got well. Streptomycin injections were prescribed for her, one meal for five days, B-complex, including septrin antibiotic tablets of two in the morning and night. Multivitamin C tablets and cough syrup were also administered for five days. The doctor further advised that Ugomma should avoid eating fried food and exposing her body. While in admission, Ugomma became quite familiar and friendly with the nursing sisters, who prayed and counselled her about being more spiritually inclined and walking closely with God, her Creator, in order to actualise her very essence in life.

'Look, Ugomma, my dear, the best approach to understanding life is spiritual instinct said Sister A. B Chung.

'Beauty without the knowledge and fear of God is vanity. Above the physical, what matters most is the beauty of the soul. For it is this inner beauty of the soul that radiates and attracts goodness to the person. You see, my friend Ugomma, now God has heard our prayers and has healed you. Tomorrow morning, hopefully the doctor will discharge you and probably we may not see you again, but bear this in mind and meditate upon it always. People who believe, accept, and act the ordinary never get far in life. Because it is the "extra" that launches one to the high echelon of indelible success,' said Sister Ebelebe.

'Sisters, I am grateful on how you two have taken good care of me these past four days I have been here. Maybe it is by design that I met with you people on this trip. All the same, may I know the identification of the symbol on your chest?'

'Well, Ugomma,' answered Sister Ebelebe, 'this symbol is the badge of The World International Sacred Peace Movement, a Christian body or, preferably, a paragon prodigious church that is found on a universal love and enjoys the same. We have branches all over the country and all over the world, working towards the benefits of mankind as Christ Jesus is our Lord, Saviour, and King now and for eternity.'

'That is interesting, Sister, and I must confess that you two have affected me with your great love, and this I will remember all through my life.'

'Ugomma, my dear, God bless and be with you, goodbye,' said

Sister Chung. And Sister Ebelebe handed Ugomma a hand bill which contained the following verse:

> If there is Right in the Soul,
> There will be Beauty in the Person
> And if there is Beauty in the Person,
> There will be Harmony in the Home
> And if there's Harmony in the Home,
> There will be Order in the Nation,

And if there is Order in the Nation,
There will be Peace in the World.

The next morning at 9 a.m., Dr Beatrus came to the hospital and discharged Ugomma. It was Wednesday, the week after they had got to the city. Of course, Fatima was happy that Ugomma was well again and hearty. Hence, that morning she chartered a taxi to drive Ugomma home, since her father went to keep an appointment with a business partner, which was unavoidable. Invariably, they arrived home about 10 a.m. The children had all gone to school at that time of the morning. 'Fatima, when are we returning back to Uyo?'

'Ugo dear, I think the weekend will be all right,' suggested Fatima. 'More so, you need some time to fully recuperate before we can conveniently travel.'

'Even at that, I suggest we fly back through Calabar,' said Ugomma.

Haba, Ugo! That will be too expensive?

'Not to worry, Fati, I'll foot the bill. That will save us the hassles of travelling by road?

'Okay, Ugo, that will make the journey faster? Consequently, they agreed to travel on Saturday instead of the earlier scheduled Sunday.

That evening the entire Yusuf family was happy that their August visitor was well again. Mrs Halima Yusuf prepared a special dinner for them to celebrate Ugomma's speedy recovery, which was a special miracle, because a lot of first timers to Jos during this period became ill as she did and died before adequate medical care was administered to them; once they started coughing and vomiting blood, that was the end. Hence, there was every cause to celebrate Ugomma's recuperation to good health.

After this time out, however, Fatima informed her parents about their rescheduled plan to travel on Saturday, which was three days away, instead of Sunday. For the remaining two days, Mrs Yusuf put her daughter and Ugomma on a special diet. Mr Yusuf, although a very busy man who left home in the morning and came back late in the evening, still made out time to share love and care with his family, specifically during the morning devotion and night benediction.

On Friday morning around 9.55 a.m., Miriam arrived home to see Fatima and Ugomma. 'Who's in here?' she called out, stepping into Fatima's living room.

'Yes! Come on in responded Fatima. 'Ah! That is you, Miriam. How're you doing?'

'Very well. Please, where's your friend, Ugomma?'

'She's taking her bath,' replied Fatima.

In fact, I'm sorry I was unable to come over as expected over the last weekend. We had a visiting lecturer from Israel, who was on sabbatical leave. The man is a workaholic and engaged us all through the day after your visit till yesterday. Although it has been quite hectic, we enjoyed working with him.'

At this juncture, Ugomma walked into the sitting room, radiating wonderful good health and confidence. 'There you're, Miriam. Nice to see you again,' she greeted her. Miriam was perplexed wondering if this was the same Ugomma she had met the week before. After the sickness, Ugomma seemed to have found peace within; plus with the marvellous motherly care of Mrs Yusuf and the uninterrupted rest which she had been enjoying, the sparkling beauty of Ugomma now captivated all around her.

'Hi, Ugomma she eventually responded. I'm sorry I couldn't keep up with our date. I was explaining to Fatima before you came in about the visiting lecturer we had from Israel the next day after your visit, who engaged us in marathon lectures till yesterday.'

'There's no problem, Miriam. It was even better you never did. I was hospitalised for pneumonia at the Nigerian Air Force Hospital.'

'What! You don't mean it?' exclaimed Miriam.

'You mean Fati has not told you yet?'

'Not yet, Ugo,' responded Fatima. 'It's not long a time since she arrived.'

'Well, here we are,' said Ugomma. 'Tomorrow I shall bid goodbye to this Tin City, for who knows when—may be for life. I've actually enjoyed myself, despite the ill health. I even thank God for it. It availed me the opportunity of meeting two important persons at the hospital, who have affected my life positively.'

'You mean those Nursing Sisters Chung and Ebelebe?' Fatima asked.

'Yes, my dear. They are wonderful rare gems. I'll forever remember them and their good works. You need to hear them singing when they are not busy with routine services. Their melodious tunes were so rhapsodic on the second evening of my admission that I forgot the pains and drifted into a deep sound sleep. The consonance filtered into my soul that the next morning I felt completely healed, but I had to remain there for proper rest and closer observations.'

'Well, Ugomma, you see, I honour my promise,' said Miriam, arranging the canvass on the standing chisel in the centre of the room. 'Let's have your painting now.'

'That's all right, Miriam. I'm excited about this. How do you want me to pose?' Ugomma asked. Miriam expertly arranged the portal flowers into a heart shape and placed a chair in the midst, and after a thorough observation and satisfied with the scene she had created, she asked Ugomma to sit in there, but sideways. Fatima watched keenly; within forty-five minutes, the picture looked stunning.

'Ugomma, come and have a look,' implored Miriam. Ugomma and Fatima were delightfully surprised at the ingenuity and classical masterpiece Miriam had produced within a short time. 'Anyway, Ugo, the painting is not going to be ready by tomorrow as you both are departing for Uyo. But don't worry. After completing the work and framing it, I can DHL it to you, that is, if you can't wait till after this second semester vacation when Fatima will hopefully be returning to the campus, the next academic year.'

'No, no! Mimi! I'll love to have it next week through the courier service before we actually go on vacation. This is the greatest and invaluable souvenir I'll present to my parents when I return back to Lagos for the holiday. And how much do you think the courier company will charge for the postage?'

'I cannot say precisely, but may be within the range of 500 naira only said Miriam.

'Well, that is no big deal,' said Ugomma, as she walked inside the house to get the money.

Lo and behold! Ugomma surprised both Miriam and her friend Fatima by giving Mimi the sum of 2,000 naira. Miriam protested, 'No, no! Ugomma, there's no need for all this much.' She returned 1,000 naira to her. But Fatima who knew Ugomma much better knew that she would never take back what she had given out.

Smiling, Fatima tapped Miriam on the shoulder and told her to keep the money, saying, 'That is Ugomma for you, and there's nothing you can do about it.'

'That's okay, Ugo. Thanks for being generous.' Ugomma handed a neatly written address to Miriam while she was packing her materials into the bag, ready to return back to the campus. Then at exactly 12.15 p.m.

they all walked outside the compound, at the roadside, and stopped a taxi that would take Miriam back.

'Where are you going to?' the driver asked.

'Campus replied Miriam. The driver in response opened the passenger door for her, and she got in, waving at her cousin and Ugomma before the driver zoomed off. Fatima and Ugomma strolled back into the compound.

That evening, Mrs Halima Yusuf prepared a special delicacy as a farewell get-together for the entire family, as Fatima and Ugomma would be departing on the flight early the next morning. It was a memorable night for Ugomma, especially spending time with the children who fondly called her Sister Bature. After dinner, Fatima's parents went into their room. Ugomma gathered the children and gave each of them 100 naira and also informed them about her departure the next morning, and they all thanked her and wished her well. The same night, she and Fatima packed their light luggage and tidied up Fatima's room, because they would not be able to do the same in the morning.

After the morning devotion at five thirty on Saturday, 29 May, Ugomma and Fatima prepared to depart Jos the Tin City, back to Uyo. Mr Yusuf would drop them off at the airport before travelling to Kaduna on a business trip that morning. 'Mama, thank you for everything. I'm indeed grateful and may God bless you all said Ugomma to Mrs Yusuf.

'You're welcome, my daughter, and God bless you too she responded. 'Fatima, you two should take good care of yourselves and face your studies seriously.'

'Okay Mama, thanks and good-bye responded Fatima and Ugomma.

'Good bye, children Ugomma said.

They responded, 'Goodbye, Sister Bature.' They all laughed at the nickname and the sense of humour of the children.

'Okay, ladies, shall we be on our way?' declared Mr Yusuf, picking up his briefcase. They all moved into the outer compound and into the car, after they stocked their bags into the boot of the car, then drove off to the airport.

Within forty-five minutes of time, they reached the airport. Mr Yusuf dropped the girls and continued on to his journey to Kaduna. Subsequently, Ugomma and Fatima bought their tickets and boarded the plane, which took off by 10 a.m. As the plane gained altitude and they were airborne, Ugomma looking down from her window said, 'Peace be still', and Fatima responded, 'Amen.'

Chapter Eight

Ugomma and Fatima arrived in Uyo about 5 p.m. It was 29 May the same evening; their room-mates were happy to receive their sunshine Ugomma and darling Fatima back from their trip. Ugomma shared out some of the artefacts that she had bought after her visit to the zoo with Fatima as memorable souvenirs to her room-mates. 'Hi, Ugo! This trip did you a lot of good O! You look so robust and have gained some pounds observed Mercy.

'Oh, thanks, Sister Mercy. I actually had a wonderful time?

Fatima interjected, 'Hi, Mercy, what about Ogechi and Onome? Are they not back?'

'No, Fatima, don't expect them from Port Harcourt till next week.' 'Mercy, may I know if there was anyone that checked on me while we were away?' Ugomma enquired.

'Yes, Ugomma, Tony and Emeka visited thrice and dropped this note on their very last visit. Also, Mfon your friend has been anxiously expecting your return from the trip.'

'Thanks for holding the brief for us. How far are you with your project works? You must have completed that by now?

'You can say that again, Ugo. As a matter of fact, I've just collected the bound quadruplet copies from the printer and submitted them to the department through my supervisor. I'm only left with my copy right here?

'Wa woo! Mercy, you're pretty fast as if you're in a haste to run away from the system.'

'You're right, Ugo. I've had enough of this town and the campus, with a GPA of 3.86, and at least for now I need a break and should go for greener pasture soonest?

'Well, Mercy, I wish you the best of luck,' said Ugomma.

'Thanks, Ugo,' she responded.

After packing her things and keeping them in order, she changed the beddings then showered and freshened up with Fatima. She left the room in the next thirty minutes to visit Mfon. She entered Mfon's room and found her ironing her dresses. 'Hello! Mfon, my darling, how're you doing?' Ugomma greeted her.

'Hi! Sweetheart, when did you arrive?' Mfon jumped up and hugged Ugomma.

'We arrived about an hour ago.'

'Baby! You must have had a swell time over there.'

'Sure! I did after being hospitalised because of pneumonia fever.'

'Holy Jesus! Did you expose your body to cold?' Mfon asked.

'No, Mfon, after all I'm not a child. The issue is that Jos is damn chilling, especially for a first-time visitor that I was. Imagine I spent five solid days in the hospital.'

'Well, thank God you're back and healthy.'

'I thank God O!' said Ugomma while handing over the gift she had bought for her. 'So what's the current happening on campus?' asked Ugomma.

'As you should know, the student union week is winding up this weekend. Exams are starting in the next two weeks. Tony has been worried concerning you and also about the apartment stuff with regard to his landlord who is demanding for two years of advance rent. More so, he and Emeka have submitted their finished bound projects works in the appropriate quarters. Hence, with only seminar presentations and two courses to write in the exams, they are as good as having graduated.'

'What did they score in their project works?'

'Tony made an "A" while Emeka had a "B",' answered Mfon.

'That means that the duo is going to graduate with second class honours, upper division.'

'No doubt about that. I think they have worked hard enough to earn that observed Mfon.

'Well, that is great. I'm happy for them,' said Ugomma.

'Ugo, when are you seeing Tony?' Mfon asked.

'Right away. Please come along with me,' Ugomma requested. Mfon obliged her and suspended the ironing, packing the remaining dresses into her wardrobe. She then combed her hair and knotted it behind. Looking into the hung mirror on the wall, she rubbed powder, applied cologne and some make-up, and off they went. Fortunately, Tony and Emeka were at home when Mfon and Ugomma arrived there. Mfon gently knocked on the door, and

Emeka opened the door; he held it ajar for the babes to enter, smiling warmly to them. 'Ugomma, where've you been all this while?' he jokingly asked her, knowing too well that she had travelled to Jos, the last two weeks now.

Ugomma jumped on Tony, who was lying down on the bed, kissing him before Tony could utter a word of welcome. Emeka and Mfon laughed hilariously as they watched admiringly Ugomma's innocent excitement. 'Ugo, sweetheart, you left me out in the cold. You didn't even bother to come and inform me about your trip to Jos,' said Tony, teasing her.

'That's not true,' said Ugomma, protesting. 'But I asked Mfon to inform and explain to you about the urgency of our journey. And I'm sure she did just that.'

'Well, darling, stop cracking your head. You're pleasantly welcomed. The only thing is that I really missed you.'

'I also missed you all,' responded Ugomma. 'However, Mfon informed me that you were anxiously waiting for my return so that we could see the landlord.'

'Yes, of course. Most importantly, the man is outrageously demanding for a two years' advance payment,' reported Tony.

'There's no problem. It suits me better because I would not want him coming to disturb frequently.'

'I think it's proper we see him immediately further down Barracks Road, because he mentioned travelling to Port Harcourt tomorrow morning for about a month. And that is probably during the end of the exams, if not beginning of holidays.'

'That's all right, Tony. Let's go and see him,' Ugomma said.

'One more thing, Ugo, do you have the money?'

'How much is it?' she asked.

'That is 7,200 naira only?

'Okay, Tony, I've got the money with me ready.' Tony and Ugomma excused themselves from Emeka and Mfon and went downstairs. They got to the landlord's house and met him in the sitting room, where he was drinking fresh palm wine with a visitor.

'Good evening, sir,' Tony and Ugomma greeted him.

'You are both welcome,' he responded.

'Sir, here's my sister Ugomma, about whom I told you regarding taking over the apartment.'

'I see!' the landlord responded. Staring at Ugomma, he belched, before speaking further. 'I hope your brother has told you about conditions to abide with while staying there?'

'Yes, sir,' she replied.

'And the sum involved?'

'Yes, sir,' she responded.

'Well, you are lucky. Tony is a nice boy. For his sake, I decided to ignore the pressure from other students who have been coming here. Can we now seal this arrangement, meaning the payment?' Tony handed him the money in fifty naira denominations. Counting and ascertaining that it was the total sum, the landlord wrote out a receipt still in Tony's name and handed it over to him. And they left.

Outside on the main-road as they strolled back to their apartment, Tony made an observation, 'Sweetheart, did you notice that the landlord was flirting with you already?'

'Yes, dear, so you noticed that also,' answered Ugomma.

'Why not?' replied Tony. 'So watch it before you see it coming.'

'Tony, you should've known me better than that. He dare not fumble with me, no matter in whatever guise he may employ silly strategies.'

'Well, I trust you. Am only sounding a caution.'

'Don't worry. I can perfectly handle him,' said Ugomma.

They arrived back at the house, only to find the door slightly open. They exchanged knowing glances, smiling. After a minute or two, Tony tapped on the door and waited for two minutes before quietly nudging the door inwards. Ugomma treaded in behind him; she was not surprised to see Mfon lying on top of Emeka, romantically picking his hairy chest, as they were half nude. 'How did it go, Tony?' Emeka enquired, folding his hands behind Mfon.

'I think it's rightly over now. Although some fast guys schemed to displace Ugomma's interest, that articulation is punctured, null and void. The paddy issued the receipt for payment.'

'This calls for celebration said Mfon, straightening up.

Emeka also got to his feet and brought out a half bottle of wine that was in their fridge. He poured out the contents in four glasses and handed them around, as they raised their glasses and cheered, 'Hurray! Hurray! Bravo!'

Ugomma and Mfon returned to the campus late in the evening and decided to sleep together in Ugomma's corner, with the view to gist more into the night before going to sleep.

After the student's week, the time table for exams was published and serious studies commenced. Students burnt the night lamps untiringly. Ugomma became more serious than the last semester. Her parcel arrived a week after they returned from Jos. And she displayed the painting in her bed corner. Mfon was flabbergasted to see that painting; even their matriculation picture was a far cry from the beautiful painting hanging in Ugomma's bed corner. All her roommates were excited about it, except Fatima, who was proud that her female cousin could produce such a masterpiece.

The final year students were the very first set to round up their exams, which were just a few papers. Subsequently, they started with the clearance from Library, Students Affairs division, the departments and faculties, the bursary department, and all others that required their certifications. Finally, they came to the Records and Examination units. Within a week after their exams, conventionally, the lecturers completed marking their papers and scoring them accordingly. The examination officer of each department was bestowed with the responsibility of computing the overall gross point accumulated (GPA) for the final Class of honours with the individual students will graduate with. 'Hi! Emeka, what's your final GPA?' asked Tony.

'Boy! That is 3.98. And you?'

'Well, I made 4.25.'

'That's great, brother! Our sleepless nights operated on the 1-0-1 or 0-0-1 eating routine at worst times have yielded the desired results. Oh thank God for his grace!' Emeka remarked.

'My brother, it's great and wonderful. I just feel I can fly away into the blue skies and jovially sing to God that I am grateful, like the birds happily do during summer times,' said Tony.

'The National Youth Service Corps programme, here I come,' declared Emeka.

'Where will you like to serve?' Tony asked.

'Man! Abuja, Abuja is the right place.'

'Well, for me said Tony, 'I've programmed my posting to Port Harcourt through my contact at NYSC Headquarters, Area 8. If things work out fine as planned, I'll serve with Shell PDSC.'

'Invariably, Tony, I've sealed my contact at the National Assembly complex, Three Arms Zone. That's where I'm going to solidify contacts and tutelage for a political career aimed at the next political dispensation.'

'That will be fine. Is your fiancee Mfon aware about this, your dream?'

'Oh yes! She's solidly behind me.'

'Boy! Aren't you lucky? Congratulation in all facets. We came, conquered, and bequeathed our imprints on the soil of UniUyo for academic excellence as the Vice Chancellor Professor Fola Lasisi will ever urge his students. UniUyo has offered you an understanding and supportive woman to mother your children.'

'Tony brother, I understand how you feel now, especially concerning finding a life partner. Don't rush it. Pray well over it. Surely God in his gracious time will also provide for you. Amen, I say to that. Ugomma can go and fly a kite.'

'Emeka, now that we've successfully graduated, how do you summarise your total experience here and those to be remembered?' Tony asked.

'Firstly, my brother, I've come to the conclusion that the process of graduation is more cumbersome and challenging than the euphoria of admission processes. Today, I can look back and introspectively remember fondly those that have made my stay worthwhile. To you, Tony, I say bravo. And kudos to the destiny that brought us together. Providence traded off my will and brought me to UniUyo, only to find my wife, Mfon. Now I know and I'm grateful to the patient Lord who sees the end of everything from the very beginning. The hard-earned degree will also become my password into the elite class with time. Altogether I think we're made.'

'My brother, I concur,' said Tony hilariously. 'And to Dr Okon Eminue the HOD, Dr I. Ekpe, erudite lecturer who come to class without any written material, yet delivered sound co-coordinated lectures, Dr Akan Ikpe, "you know idiosyncrasy", political powerhouse of the department, Dr Ukpe U. Ukpe, the ethical gentle friend, Dr V. B. Eno, et al., we say love and so long. And to other distinguished colleagues, Callistus I. Nnocha, Igwe Chukwuma, Rusken C. Ohuka, Clifford Thomas, Uwem Udoko, Anthony Chukwuma, Awunuga, et al., members of the National Association of Imo State Students, UniUyo Chapter, Federation of Igbo Students, the great Alumni Association of Tuskers Republic of UniUyo, we say bravo.

And so long to Dr S. N. Udoemena, Dr Ken Opara, Dr Elizabeth Nzotha, Dr Essien Essien, Dr Agbafo Igwe, the great philosopher, we say thanks and goodbye. And to Mrs C. N. Ekong, the registrar in charge of Records Department in Education Faculty, we say thanks and God bless. Dr Uwem S. Ekanem, your flair to save lives has spurred me to sincerely serve humanity through the acquisition of political power. Therefore, Doc, love and so long. And to all others we say, keep up the standard of our great alma mater, goodbye.' Like little children at play, Emeka stooped down and engraved his signature on the sands of time, giving a smile of fulfilment. Happily, Tony joined him and endorsed a dotted line and shouted 'yes' to posterity! The duo straightened up; sitting on their heels, they laughed hilariously towards the other side of life—the macro society.

Chapter Nine

Ugomma, now that the exams are over when are you returning back to Lagos?' Mfon asked.

'My sister, I'm not going to do that in a hurry, not until I've actually moved my things to the new apartment at Barracks Road. Probably fix in also a burglary proof at the door. And of course, I must have to be around for the send-off parties both for the Law Students Association department, LAWSA, and our darling friends.'

'You're right, Ugomma. Tony and Emeka surely will not compromise with our absence.'

'When is the department party coming up?' Ugomma asked.

'That should be on Friday, 26 June, which is three days away from now. And you know, it's going to be a late evening affair,' said Mfon.

'Which means that a week later, Tony and Emeka, the political juggernauts, will be celebrating their exit from this system,' observed Ugomma.

'That's life. You must get going as long as life remains replied Mfon. 'We're not stagnant waters, but being propelled by the creative force nestled in our souls by nature, emotions, ideas, aspirations, ego, and ambitions. These elements aflame the mind and get us started into actions and actualisation of set goals.'

In the few days after the LAWS A dinner party night, Ugomma started moving her belongings to the apartment at Barracks Road, her new home. 'Fatima.'

'Yes, Ugo.'

'I want to inform you that from next academic year I'll not be living in the hostel any more.'

'How do you mean, Ugomma?' Fatima asked.

'Well, I've taken over my boyfriend's apartment at Barracks Road. I've actually started moving my things gradually to that place.'

'Ugo dear, that's great. You are going to live now like a big babe.'

'Fatima, my sister, I'm fed up with this hostel routine life and inconveniencies, especially concerning my privacy.'

'Invariably, Ugo, I hope to visit you at home.' said Fatima.

'Ah! Fatima, you don't need to say that. We're always together. Even some of the things that you would not bother carrying along to Jos, you can drop and pick them up from my house when school resumes next academic year.'

'Oh thanks! It will surely save me the stress of taking them to my uncle's place at the Custom and Excise quarters at Williams Ekpenyiong Street, like the other times.'

'More so, Fatima, you're invited to the send-off party of Tony and Emeka. I and Mfon have decided to make this a special treat for them.'

'Ah! Baby, when is it happening?' Fatima asked.

'Next Tuesday, we've arranged to go for a picnic at Ibeno beach. Just for four couples. That's Tony, Emeka, and two other guys. Myself, Mfon, you, and one other babe. And I'll want you to suggest or bring another babe to complete the party.'

In that case,' said Fatima, 'I'll suggest we bring Dora, our former room-mate. She's also a fair-looking happening babe.'

'That's all right,' responded Ugomma. 'Do you know that for quite some time now I've not seen Dora? That means you've to contact her, this evening,' said Ugomma.

'Sure, that's no problem,' Fatima answered.

That evening after Sunday service, Ugomma visited Mfon in her hall and perfected their exclusive party arrangements for their pals. 'Hello! Mfon, how was your day?' Ugomma greeted her friend.

'Very well. I went to Ewet Housing Estate in the morning and joined my parents to go to Qua-Igboe Church, as they were invited for a thanksgiving ceremony of a distant relation, who just had a baby boy after eight years of marriage without any issue?

Wa-wao!' Ugomma replied. 'The couple must have gone through hell of reproach and castigations from the extended family relations?

'My sister, the story has it that even the man's old parents attempted to marry him off to a new wife on two occasions, but he rebuffed them, because he loved his wife dearly?

'Thank God for having rewarded their love and perseverance? said Ugomma.

'You should have seen the pomp and pageantry which was displayed today during the church service. It was wonderful. Well, Ugo, how's the plan going on about the picnic?'

'As far as I'm concerned, things will work out fine. I've invited Fatima and Dora, our former room-mates, to complete the number of babes for the party, and I believe that Tony and Emeka will take care of bringing two of their friends?'

'Oh, that's all right. I was thinking of the babes to join us out. What about the food and drinks?' Mfon asked.

'Well, I suggest we go and borrow two coolers from home tomorrow evening, one for drinks and the other for food.'

'You're right, Ugomma. We shall also do the cooking at your new home,' said Mfon.

'Why don't we invite Fatima and Dora to help in the cooking?' suggested Ugomma.

'That's still better,' agreed Mfon. Howbeit, at four thirty that evening, Mfon and Ugomma went to Barracks Road to inform their boyfriends about the arrangement for the Tuesday picnic.

'Hi, darling,' said Tony, as he opened the door for Ugomma and Mfon to come into the room.

Mfon sat down on the bed where Emeka was sleeping and woke him up with a tap on his shoulder. 'Hello, darling, I hope you're fine,' greeted Mfon.

'It's nice to see you this evening. I'm fine, but was taking some nap,' Emeka replied.

'I and Mfon have completed arrangements about the food matter, and we're also providing a cooler of drinks,' Ugomma narrated to Tony.

'How about the remaining two babes?' Tony asked.

'You don't need to worry about that because Fatima and Dora, our friends, have agreed to come along.'

'Oh, that is fine! That means Callistus Nnocha and Aniefor Ekong, our course mates, will also be around. Now the motor vehicle issue has been sorted out,' said Tony. 'The hired bus would take us to and from Ibeno.'

'Tony, how much did the driver charge for the trip?' Emeka asked.

'The guy demanded 1,500 naira.'

'Don't you think that that amount is exorbitant?' Mfon asked.

'Look, Tony, I think the first guy we approached is more reasonable with his charges of 1,000 naira only,' suggested Emeka.

'You know what,' said Tony, 'the guy asking for a higher amount has a newer vehicle. Therefore, I do have the assurance that he will not disappoint us on the road.' So they all agreed to hire the driver with the higher hope of efficiency, no matter the disparaging cost. Satisfied that the entire arrangements were on course, Ugomma and Mfon returned to the campus about 7.45 p.m.

As they were walking through the annex gate into the hostel grounds, Ugomma said, 'Mfon!'

'Yes, dear.'

'Is that not Dora walking through the football pitch towards the other exit gate?' Ugomma asked.

'Yes, that's her and probably with a friend of hers.'

'Come on then. Let's catch up with them suggested Ugomma.

They hastened their pace and called out to them, 'Hi, Dora! Dora, could you hold on?' said Ugomma.

'Where're you going to? I'd wanted to come over to you this evening, but thank goodness, here you are,' said Ugomma.

'I hope there's no problem,' replied Dora.

'No, my dear,' interjected Mfon. 'We're only inviting you to a picnic party next Tuesday at Ibeno beach.'

'Really?' Dora responded, not concealing her excitement. 'Thanks for remembering to invite me. Sure I'm going to be there alive. When is departure time and take-off place?' Dora asked.

'10 a.m. is the time, but you're going to join us at our boyfriends' place at Barracks Road early Tuesday morning around 7.30 to cook the food for the trip. That means you need to come over to my room at 7 a.m. so that we can all go together, okay?' said Ugomma.

'Okay, Ugo,' replied Dora. 'See you girls then.'

'Goodbye,' responded Mfon and Ugomma.

At about 7.15 a.m., Tuesday, 30 June, Fatima and Ugomma decided to pack their beach wear, other dresses, and personal effects in one bag. And immediately Dora stepped into their room with a handbag dangling over her shoulder, which was intermittently sliding off. 'Ugomma, I'm sorry that I overslept and actually woke up late this morning, thereby couldn't keep the 7 a.m. time sharp.'

'Well, Dora, there's no problem. You needed the rest. Can we now go and fetch Mfon in Hall four before proceeding to Barracks Road?' said Ugomma. And off they went.

'Hi! Mfon, I hope you're ready.'

'Yes, dear,' she replied. 'Good morning, babes,' she greeted Fati and Dora.

'Hello, Mfon!' they responded.

'Shall we go then?' said Mfon, as she picked up her bag, and they all left the room.

'Ugomma, if it's going to be difficult getting the motorbikes to carry us individually, I think it's better we ride two on each bike,' suggested Fatima.

'Yes, you're right, especially since you and Dora do not know the place. Fatima, you ride with Mfon, while I come along with Dora.'

'That's okay,' they all agreed. Eventually, they all got to their destination by 8 a.m.

'Hi! Babes, it's nice having you here. How are things with you all?' greeted Tony, as he welcomed them.

'Good morning, Tony,' they chorused. Mfon stepped inside and hugged her fiance, and they kissed each other.

'Emeka, do you remember Dora and Fatima?' Mfon asked.

'Sure, I recognised their faces as your room-mates from the last session, although I can't remember their names except now that you called them,' replied Emeka. 'Well, Dora, it's nice meeting you again,' he said, stretching out his hands to shake hers.

'It's nice to meet you also,' replied Dora, shaking his hand.

'Of course, Fatima, you were forever there with Ugomma, whenever I and Tony visited.'

'Yes, Emeka, congratulations for your graduation,' responded Fatima.

'Thanks, my dear,' said Emeka.

Without much ado about protocols, the babes busied themselves with the cooking, and by 9.30 a.m. they had completed all that. They packed the chilled drinks in the cooler and were set to go. Fifteen minutes later, Callistus and Aniefork got to the place. 'Oh come on! What's delaying Tony?' Ugomma asked, worried. 'It is 10.15 a.m. already.'

'My sister, it may be that the bus driver has fucked up responded Mfon.

'That wouldn't be funny at all. Not when we've given him advance payment of 500 naira said Emeka.

'Well, here they come observed Mfon as the vehicle parked in front of the compound, and Tony came out.

'Hi, good folks he called out to them standing in the balcony. 'Shall we go?' They all rushed down, carrying the two coolers into the parked vehicle.

'Man, you stayed longer than expected observed Emeka.

'My brother, the driver went on another charter to Ibafon Army Barracks, necessitating me to wait for him at the park to return.'

'Well, thank God we can still keep the date said Emeka. They all entered the vehicle, and the driver sped off. After passing Ibom roundabout, he headed towards Aka Road. Then he gathered more momentum and accelerated to Eket.

They eventually got to Qua Ibeno beach at 12.05 p.m. Coincidentally, they reached QIT Mobil gate beside the only entrance to the beach. This was because the Mobil Producing Unlimited developed, monitored, and regularised the usage of this beach; hence, all visitors had to park their vehicles at the Mobil car park before strolling further down to the seashore. As Ugomma and her party were alighting from the bus and carrying their luggage down, a car going out from the gate horned constantly to attract their attention. As the babes turned towards the car, Ugomma immediately recognised the car and the person behind the wheels.

Daniel Stephen parked his Benz 190E car and came out, leaving the door ajar. He leant on it, staring at Ugomma and her friends. Not only did Ugomma instantaneously have a flashback, her roommate, Fatima, also recognised Daniel as the person who had visited their room with Ugomma that fateful Sunday evening last semester. 'Ugomma, is that not that guy who accompanied you to the hostel one particular Sunday evening?' Fatima asked.

'Yes, he's Mr Daniel Stephens.'

'What's he doing here?' Fatima asked.

'He works with Mobil,' responded Ugomma.

'Forget him, Ugomma. Look, Tony and the other guys are watching and probably wondering what's going on,' said Mfon.

They eventually turned and walked towards the beach, trailing behind the guys. Daniel was seeing Ugomma now after the incident last semester. He started reminiscing about the escapades he had enjoyed with Ugomma and desired to have her again, although his conscience started pricking him as to why he had not bothered checking on her ever since. After all, Ugomma had been nice to him and had every reason to have kept him incommunicado after getting the abortion done because of him. His brows knit, he drove off to Eket town, wishing to meet Ugomma again at the soonest and apologise for neglecting her for this long gap in time.

The party was gay and full of great fun, with pictures being snapped, dancing, and food. Tony was waiting for a convenient time to take Ugomma aside and ask her the question that had been bothering his mind since that moment they arrived at the beach. Although uncertainty about what would be Ugomma's reaction had been keeping him in check, yet he was resolute to extract the truth from Ugomma. After all, what has he to gain or lose, especially, since Ugomma had refused to marry him? Then came the moment he had been expecting. As the others carried on dancing, he manoeuvred Ugomma beside the boot, where they leant, then he confronted her with the question. 'Ugomma!'

'Yes, dear,' she answered him.

'Although it does not matter, but may I know who was that guy who rudely caught our attention as soon as we disembarked from the bus some hours ago?'

Ugomma, who was not surprised by Tony's inquisition, had already prepared her answer. 'Well, Daniel is a friend of mine.'

'How and when did you know him?' Tony asked.

At this juncture, Ugomma took offence, but she restrained herself hard not to flare up at the slightest provocation. She answered, 'Look, Tony, I think you're infringing on my right as an individual. Why don't we drop this matter and enjoy this moment while it lasts?' She playfully dragged Tony by his hands towards the party. Tony had no choice or chance with Ugomma, but he had to accept the things the way they are and followed her back to the party. The party ended at 4.20 p.m. and they boarded the vehicle, and the driver who had enjoyed himself with them got behind the wheels and engaged the engine which roared, as he pressed down the throttle, lodged the gear, and off they went back to Uyo. The vehicle went straight to the campus to drop off Dora, Fatima, Calistus, and Enefiok before dropping off Tony, Emeka, Ugomma, and Mfon at Barracks Road. He exchanged pleasantries with them before the vehicle drove off.

When they arrived, Emeke said, 'Mfon, my darling, and Ugomma, I want to express our profound gratitude to you babes for the success of this outing. Tony, I hope I'm speaking your mind also?'

'Yes, my brother, go ahead?'

'You see, it's not an easy thing to have friends who truly care, even ready to sacrifice time and resources for other people's pleasure and well-being. Hence, we appreciate and pray that the good Lord will reward both of you. One other thing is that few days from now I and Tony shall be departing this town, and of course, we will be visiting you babes from time to time. Invariably, my advice is that you should be very studious and work hard to achieve the very essence of academic excellence.'

'Thanks, Emeka. We wish you guys all the very best out there,' responded the two ladies.

'Well, good friends, Emeka has actually summarised it all. Nevertheless, in a nutshell, my advice is that you both should continue to work as a team, especially academically, for that will enhance and facilitate your excelling, especially as course mates. That really helped I and Emeka. No doubt we shall be visiting you from time to time as Emeka has earlier said.'

'Thanks, Tony, we shall actually be missing you guys.' Ugomma and Mfon decided to take the coolers back to Mfon's home at Ewet Housing Estate.

'Tony, we should be getting to Ewet Housing Estate before it gets late?

'Okay, Ugo, when do we see you again?' asked Tony.

'Have you forgotten that your departmental send-off party is on 3 July, in the next three days?' Ugomma asked.

'You know as well as I do that that is not what I mean.'

'Okay, Tony, when are you expecting me?' she asked. Tony drew her more close and whispered to her that Emeka would be visiting the Ekongs the next morning around 10 a.m. 'Okay, that settles it. See you then.'

'Okay, good night,' responded Tony.

The couples walked downstairs to stand by the roadside. 'Emeka, remember that my parents are expecting you tomorrow by 10 a.m.'

'Darling, you know I would not forget that,' Emeka reassured Mfon. The cyclists pulled up and the girls climbed on them, and they drove off into the star-studded twinkling night skies.

On the morrow, Ugomma took a long deliberate bath, carefully applied make-up and cologne, and selected a smart gown, which although made her feel free it conjured up an appealing posture which she knew would provoke Tony sensually. She also deliberately wore the same kind of coloured bra and panties which she wore the day she visited Richard and sold off her virginity. She brushed her long hair behind and knotted it with a ribbon, looking titivating. She got to the apartment by 10.05 a.m. by which time Emeka would have gone to his prospective in-laws. 'Hello, Tony she greeted him without knocking on the open door.

'Hi, Ugo he responded with wide open arms and hugged her. Planting a kiss on her red lips, he asked, 'Welcome, darling, how was your night?'

'Well, fine, I slept like a baby. An uninterrupted sleep it actually was till early this morning, when I went outside and eased myself.'

'What do I offer you? Food?' Tony asked.

'No, please, I indeed had a full breakfast an hour ago. A drink will suffice.'

'Okay then, you can finish the remaining Baccus wine left in the fridge.' He poured out the drink in a glass and handed it over to her.

'Take a sip Ugomma urged him, as she held out the cup to his mouth. He obliged, swallowed softly while watching her face.

Ugomma gulped the remaining contents in a straight swallow, then coughed softly, which brought tears in her eyes. The effect reflected in her dazzling brown eyes and kindled her libido. Although Tony was excited and fond of this enigmatic babe, yet he could not elucidate the actions and intricacies of her personality. 'Tony, can you luck that door?' Ugomma requested. He obliged and put on the CD player with the music of Alex O's 'My Banana'. At other times, men had initiated sex with her, but here and now this morning, Ugomma assumed that initiative, maybe to assert her right as a full-fledged human being. 'Tony, do you know that women need men more than men do?'

'I wouldn't say that,' he responded. 'Not with all the hullabaloo about sex abuse of the womenfolk.'

'Forget that, darling. My gender is mostly pretenders when it comes to the issue of sex, especially in this part of the world where sex is treated as sacrilege, yet fornication and adultery has become the order of day.' Subsequently, they made love, then relaxed with lots of gist till she was ready to go. They strolled downstairs titillated. They climbed the same bike and returned to the campus; stopping at the main campus gate, they paid off the cyclist and walked into the campus. Walking hand in hand, they reached the convocation park that was deserted at that time of the evening. They continued to gist till 9 p.m. before Tony escorted her back to her hostel on the annex campus. Before 3 July, Ugomma had practically moved into her apartment at Barracks Road and only passed the nights at the hostel.

Minor renovation works had been done in the apartment according to her taste. The wardrobe had been fixed; burglary proofs to the door and windows were securely in place. She also repainted the room to a cream colour and added brown curtains and a red rugged carpet. Other home accessories like television, CD player, she hoped to bring in the next academic year. As Tony had decided leaving his fridge behind as a parting gift, she therefore did not need to bother about a new one.

'Ugomma!'

'Yes, Tony?'

'I want you to put on your best clothes for this party. I hope to make my last social outing on this campus as an undergraduate the most memorable.'

'Yea, Tony, you can say that again as if I'm not involved. You don't worry but leave that to me. Or have you forgotten that I'm yet to be crowned queen of UniUyo?' They both laughed, holding each other's hand joyously.

Akwa Ibom's magnificent hall was the venue, along I. B. Babangida Bourlivia, off downtown Aka Road. The hall was filling up with distinguished celebrants, bigwigs of the departmental staff, invited guests, members of the student's union, government, and other people. Tony and Ugomma got to the venue in a chartered taxi at 7.5 5 p.m. and paid off the driver. He was dressed in a grey-coloured three piece suit, a sparkling white shirt, a red tie, and the maroon shoes that Ugomma had bought for him after the first semester holidays. Clean shaved and with a haircut, Tony looked smashingly handsome, and Ugomma looked breathtaking beautiful. She deliberately flaunted her newly set long hair to loosely rest on her shoulders. Her dazzling brown eyes which were her greatest asset tantalised everyone around. She was wearing that same brown gown that her mother had bought for her in London for her seventeenth birthday. Instead of black shoes and bag, she wore the same maroon coloured shoes and bag to match Tony's. She had added a light make-up, which enhanced her beautiful oval face. And the designer perfume she wore also filtered around her and left a trailing smell wherever she turned to. The effect and appearance of Tony and Ugomma was stunning. They became the cynosure of all eyes. Emeka and his fiancee, Mfon, also got there a couple of minutes later. Calistus and his fiancee, Tina, also arrived later.

'Hi, Tony and Ugomma, you are looking gorgeously wonderful greeted Emeka and Mfon.

'Hello, good friends responded Tony, as Ugomma hugged her friend Mfon. And they all moved towards Calistus, Tony Chuks, and the rest of the colleagues.

'Hello, Calistus, how is it going?' greeted Emeka.

'Welcome, gentlemen and ladies he responded and introduced his fiancee Tina, who had come in from the Institute of Management and Technology, Enugu, to grace the occasion. They all exchanged pleasantries and walked into the hall, after snapping photographs.

Finally, the special guest of honour, Obong Victor Atah, the governor of the state, who was a distinguished colleague of political science, also arrived in the company of the HOD, Dr Okon Eminue, and other paraphernalia of government functionaries, which included three principal officers of the state assembly, who were also great Tuskers.

The party kicked off in earnest at 8.50 p.m. with the welcome address from the HOD. The governor also read his speech and bid the graduates farewell. A few minutes later, after opening the dancing floor, the special guest of honour and his entourage departed. The jamboree commenced and lasted till the early hours of the next day.

Tony, Emeka, Ugomma, and Mfon left the venue in a hired taxi back to their home at Barracks Road. They arrived there by 4.45 a.m. and paid off the driver. 'Boy, what a fulfilling night!' declared Tony.

'My brother, it has been worthwhile,' Emeka responded. They entered their room and continued the celebration with a toast, dancing for the next thirty minutes before they slept.

Eventually, they all woke up at 9.45 a.m. 'Good morning, ladies and gentleman!' Emeka greeted.

'Fine morning, my brother,' responded Tony, stretching out his entire frame and yawning hungrily. 'Hi, babes, shall we have breakfast, please?'

'Darling, take it easy. We're exhausted as well,' replied Ugomma. 'Mfon, how has it been with you?' Ugomma enquired.

'Fine, sweetheart, let's fix up breakfast for these guys. I know they will be this hungry this early after the quantity of beer they consumed last night?

Invariably, they all enjoyed the fried plantains and eggs, custard, and Milo beverage. Mfon and Ugomma bathed together, while Tony and Emeka did the same. That afternoon around 2 p.m., Tony and Emeka left the town for Owerri. And Ugomma prepared to depart the next day back for Lagos, after tidying up the entire apartment. 'Mfon, I hope you'll come around to see me off tomorrow afternoon.'

'Oh, sure, Ugo. After getting home this evening, I'll be with you first thing tomorrow about 9 a.m.' That night on 4 July, Ugomma packed only two travelling bags of the things she'd need in Lagos and the clothes she would not need any more. The other items she secured them in the wardrobe and slept off.

On the morrow, 5 July, Mfon got to Ugomma's apartment at 8.5 5 a.m. 'Sweetheart, how was the night?' she greeted Ugomma.

'My dear, I had a disturbing dream which is bugging my mind since the early morning.'

'What's it all about?' Mfon asked, sounding concerned.

'Mfon, my sister, a handsome little boy was crying and following me about, calling me "Mother" in the dream.'

'Oh, mine! Ugo, dear, what've you got to do with that that it should transcend into reality and disturb your peace of mind?' Mfon asked.

'You don't understand, Mfon.' She sat dejectedly on the bed, rubbing her hands together and looking pensive. Mfon then sat near her and threw her hands around Ugomma's neck, consolingly, wishing

Ugomma could speak up and offload the burden in her heart. 'Mfon, my sister, do you remember the incident that occurred when we arrived at Qua Ibeno beach last week?'

'Yes, Ugo. Do you mean that friend of yours, Daniel?'

'Yes, that last semester when we had a misunderstanding and I was not regular in class, it was at the very climax of my truancy and folly with him.'

'How do you mean?' Mfon queried.

'Eventually, I became pregnant from him and aborted the baby,' responded Ugomma and started crying profusely.

'Holy Lord!' Mfon shouted. 'You did what? You committed abortion last semester, Ugo?' Mfon queried, sorrowfully. Ugomma could not restrict herself any more and hide the secrets lodged in her mind. And for once, she shared her burden with a loving and caring friend, who would not ridicule her misdemeanour for hours. 'Well, I'm sorry, Ugo, but you didn't listen or heed my advice then, of settling down with Tony and forgetting other men and their sweet nonsense deceits. Look at the mess you've landed yourself now.'

'Mfon, do you know the worst thing bothering me now is what the faculty will do to me, when we resume next session, concerning the carry-overs I had the first semester?'

'Well, Ugomma, your guess is as good as mine. Let time decide that,' said Mfon.

'I've to go now,' said Ugomma finally. She locked up the apartment and they carried her two big pieces of luggage, while she hung the handbag over her shoulder. Then they both strolled up to the ADC Airline booking office at No 1, Barracks Road. After buying her ticket and tagging her luggage, she stood outside with Mfon, gist, before the rest of the passengers came out to board the coaster bus that would transport them to Calabar Airport. She hugged Mfon, and they both kissed goodbye.

Chapter Ten

The irreparable damage that was done in the second year, first semester, became the very bane that shattered Ugomma's law career in the University of Uyo. Even if she passed her second semester courses with flying colours, accumulating 3.65 GPA, the woeful failed courses of the first semester and the carry-over disaster, dimmed her studentship rainbow and utterly cast a gloom over her joy and aspirations. The University of Uyo amongst other tertiary institutions in Nigeria strove to uphold and maintain the high standards of the Nigerian University Commission. Therefore, before Ugomma returned back from vacation, there was a notice on the information board requesting her to see the dean of the law faculty as soon as possible.

Mfon came around to check up the enlisted course outline for the new 300 level courses so that she could fill and register for the new session, only to discover the notice. She felt so bad and walked away dejectedly. Ugomma was intelligent enough, but allowed herself to become distracted and lost focus. And now this notice was nothing but rustication. Mfon was so drenched in this rumbling thought in her mind while walking away that she failed to notice another course mate, Ezekiel, who was greeting her.

That weekend, on 10 October, being a Saturday, Ugomma returned to Uyo. After settling down and putting her apartment in order, she decided to visit Mfon at home in Ewet Housing Estate. Hence, she arrived there at 5.30 p.m. and entered the compound. Mfon, who was relaxing in the balcony upstairs, saw her and rushed down to welcome her. 'Hello, sweetheart, when did you arrive?' Mfon asked as they walked into the house.

'This afternoon,' answered Ugomma. 'And how are you all faring?'

'Fine,' replied Mfon. 'Only that I am lonely. My parents travelled to Eket to visit Granny with Ntekpere.'

'Come off it! Here are the presents from my parents to you all.'

'Oh thanks, my dear. I hope they're all fine, and the business empire?'

'Yes, my sister, there's no problem. Uchendu specifically sent his regards.'

'Ah, Uche, my darling, which class is he now?' Mfon asked.

'He's in senior secondary year three. And Maarako has just gotten admission into the University of Nigeria Nsukka to study medicine and surgery?

Wa-wao! That's great, Ugomma. My dear, thank God for them?

'Yea, Mfon, have you been to the campus since the resumption?'

'Yes, of course, I went to get the new course outline and probably register for the new session yesterday. Actually I saw a notice on the information board requesting you to see the dean as soon as possible?

Ugomma heaved out a sigh before responding. 'Well, that's it. The die is cast,' she said stoically. After spending some more minutes with Mfon, she departed back for her home after Mfon promised visiting and spending Sunday night with her so that they both would go to the campus together on Monday morning 12 October at 11.05 a.m. Ugomma knocked and walked into the dean's office and greeted him, 'Good morning, sir?

'Fine morning, my dear. What can I do for you?' he responded, looking up from his desk, straight into Ugomma's face, assessing her.

'Sir, I am Ugomma Uboma, a now part three student of this faculty. I saw a notice on the information board requesting me to see you as soon as possible?

'I see!' responded the grey-headed Professor Etuk Udo Umoh, as he pulled out a file from his cabinet and handed Ugomma a letter, duly signed by him.

Look, dear, I can't understand what went wrong in your career in the first semester year two. It's unbelievable that after doing so well in year one, you slid into oblivion in the subsequent semester, failing all your courses. However, at the faculty board meeting, we decided on a minimum punitive measure of rusticating you for a session instead of total expulsion from the system, with the view that you would have sorted yourself out properly and probably expunged yourself off the libido and juvenile delinquency that has caused the upset in your noble career. This other letter is for your parents, and I do hope that you will ensure giving it to them, when you reach home. Good luck and goodbye.'

With that final word, he dismissed Ugomma from his office. Mfon, who had been waiting outside for her friend, observed pitiably as Ugomma came out of the dean's office with her shoulders hunched, red-eyed, and sobbing convulsively. Mfon rushed to her rescue, offering a handkerchief. 'Ugo darling, try to compose yourself and not draw attention to yourself.

People will not come to cheer, but mock you. So be yourself and let's get out of this place,' counselled Mfon.

Ultimately, they decided to return to Ugomma's house on Barracks Road. 'Ugomma, what're you going to do now?' Mfon asked, downcast.

'My sister, I'm just confused and do not know where to start picking up my pieces. In fact, I'm at sea,' replied Ugomma.

'If I may advise, Ugo, I'll suggest you go home to Lagos and inform your parents about this latest development.'

'What?!' she screamed. 'I dare not do that, because my father's proud heart will be aflame. Mfon, I've confided in you about all my travails, and that suffices for now. My Parents need not know about this for now, because I'm going to keep them in cloud cuckoo land until this problem's over. After all, the rustication is for one session.'

Mfon became bemused at the utterance of her friend, shaking her head. 'No, no! Ugomma, you can never tell. Your father could do something positive about this situation or even send you overseas to complete the academics there?

'Rather? She laughed blithely, tapping Mfon on the shoulder. 'Chill, my sister, thank goodness I've got this apartment. I can come and go at will without anyone bothering into my affairs, except you Mfon? From that moment, Mfon knew that things would never be the same again between them, because definitely Ugomma was going to assume another life pattern and probably jive around more to jettison this year of the plundering wastage.

Three weeks later, when the academics had fully blossomed, the penultimate semester's results were published, and Mfon consolidated her good GPA. Even Ugomma's results surprised Mfon because Ugomma made A's and B's in her courses, with only a C in a paper. That evening, she rushed to Barracks Road to inform Ugomma about it, only to be greeted by the securely locked up apartment, because Ugomma had travelled to Port Harcourt to visit her maternal uncle. In the middle of November, quite unconventionally, Ugomma flew back to Lagos, spent a week, and returned to Uyo. Her parents were unsuspecting about the rationale behind her mid-semester homecoming and never asked her. She spent the remaining part of the semester travelling and visiting distant relations in other towns and cities. And finally she went back to Lagos for the Xmas holidays. Eventually, Emeka visited Uyo during that period before the Xmas holidays to see his fiancee Mfon.

'Hi, my darling! How're you coping with the National Youth Service Corps programme?' Mfon asked Emeka.

'My dear, Abuja is pretty cool. There's no problem he replied while sipping his Stout beer. 'Mfon, let's get you another bottle of malt drink, okay?'

'Well, I wouldn't mind,' she said. 'Have you been in contact with your friend, Tony?'

'Oh sure! He's doing fine in Port Harcourt,' replied Emeka. 'Moreover, Tony informed me that he has won the American Visa Lottery, in the latest result released last week of November.'

'Good God,' shouted Mfon. 'No, it's a lie! Sweetheart, please stop this joke.'

'Oh come off it! Mfon, I'm serious. His cousin in the United States actually phoned him about the cheering news.'

'Imagine that! Ugomma has missed out.'

'That reminds me, where's Ugomma?' Emeka enquired.

'My dear, it's wonderful and unbelievable that Ugomma of all people has been rusticated from the faculty.'

'What!' Emeka exclaimed. 'What went wrong and where's the point of departure?'

'Beloved, Ugomma messed up her second year first semester with a total failure in all the courses, and your guess is as good as mine?'

'What do the consequences entail and where's she now?' Emeka further asked.

'Honestly, I don't know about her movements now. Moreover, she comes around once in a while.'

'O mine! What a *brainless beauty!* Tony must hear this?

'Well, Emeka, do you know that she made a better result last semester than me?'

'Are you serious? But why this rustication, oh why?'

'Look, Emeka, I feel really sorry for my friend, Ugomma, because as the saying goes, "It's easier to go astray, but difficult to reconstruct". She even refused to inform her parents about this development,' concluded Mfon. Poor her, the brainless beauty; she threw caution to the wind and harvested the whirlwind.

The End.